BOY
WITHOUT A
FATHER

HOW EXTRATERRESTRIALS INFLUENCE
US/CONTACT AND REINCARNATION IN A
REMOTE ANDEAN VILLAGE

PAUL W NARAGON

outskirts
press

Outskirts Press, Inc.
http://www.outskirtspress.com

ISBN: 978-1-9772-5666-9

PREFACE

A growing interest in outer space is undeniable. But more to the point Earthlings are fascinated with the growing prospects of the existence of intelligent life forms on planets in other star systems as is evidenced by the fact that they're coming here! They've been coming periodically for thousands of years. The evidence is indisputable, further suggesting the textbook's understanding of our evolution is misleading and incomplete.

While written as fiction, BOY WITHOUT A FATHER, is a remembered account of an actual event that occurred in the 13th Century in a remote mountain village on the Eastern slope of the Andes in South America when extraterrestrials from a planet in the Sirius Star System made contact.

The journeyers from Sirius are on a mission to facilitate the evolution of those they contact. The contact is not at all random, but intentional.

In this story, they contacted villagers of a remote Andean Mountain village bringing a gift, a human baby, a boy, who was to be raised as one of the Quechua villagers' own, making this contact the entry point into the reincarnation cycle on Earth for the spirit of this boy.

As suggested, the child from space is not the first of its kind. The Sirians have participated in countless instances of such "Starseed drops" on what they call the Blue Planet in a manner so clever and indirect as to influence the spiritual development of its inhabitants delicately. There is little doubt that many humans on Earth today had their origin as spirits who have come from other star systems to influence the course of human evolution on this planet and participate in their evolutionary development.

"Drops" are a means the Sirians use to comply with the fundamental law in the galaxy, which is non-interference. The mandate deals primarily with interaction between spacefaring civilizations and non-spacefaring, stating the former should not interfere in the latter's development without adequate cause.

The "Down to Earth" narrative proceeds through the first life of this boy on Earth as he grows into adulthood, the fantastic things he does and says to help transform the lives of the villagers, which comes to a shocking climax and reiterates that life is without end.

1

An unusually hot dry-season night in the small and remote village of Sonqollaqta high on the eastern flank of the Andes mountains, where the nights were generally cold to a harsh degree, this night was an unbelievable exception for the villagers. Yet, another exception, more profound and consequential, was about to occur. Visitors arriving from out of town, strangers from out of this world.

Due to the exceptionally balmy temperature, most villagers had shed their heavy garments normally worn, built cooking fires outside rather than inside to prepare meals as a way of enjoying nature's invitation to be outdoors. The change invigorated the villagers.

Near the middle of the village, a young couple in their early twenties, Arisi, the man, and Kuychi, the woman, married going on two years, were seated outside on camelid skins, nestling in each other's arms. As they leaned back and were resting comfortably, Kuychi looked skyward and said —

"Such an unusually warm evening. This high in the mountains, the nighttime temperature constantly freezes standing water, but look, the sky is cloudless, and the temperature has not dropped."

"Yes, my love," her husband, who had a charming disposition and was more focused on her, replied, "I see the far away sparkling gems of Mayu (the Milky Way), which would go well around your neck, adding a dazzling look to your appearance."

Kuychi, in her turquoise sweater and traditional black skirt, blushed in response. Arisi smiled, then kissed her.

To Arisi, Kuychi was a beauty. She was slimmer than most other Quechuan women, had a narrow youthful face, framed nicely by long, straight black hair; her shiny brown eyes were large and her lips thick. Her appearance was inviting to her husband; something other men in the village told Arisi.

Both feeling aroused, they gathered the things they had laid out and retired to the privacy of their house.

The amorous couple quickly undressed and sat on the edge of the bed, kissing. Then the two lovers lay naked in the bed beside each other, enjoying the warm breeze coming in the door, rather than cold air as was usual. But to their surprise, their desired sexual fantasy would never come to fruition, and it wasn't because of lack of trying. Instead, just when the breathing was getting heavier and their fleshy bodies intermingled, there was yelling outside.

Kuychi and Arisi stopped and listened, wondering what was going on. Listening intently for a moment, Arisi recognized the voices, "It's the Gang of Four in the thicket," then added with a tone of irritation, "Not the first time and certainly won't be the last we'll hear of their craziness." He had no interest in pursuing the disruption any further. His eyes were on something more promising. Besides, Arisi was aware that drinking Killa k'anchay made people crazy and talk nonsense. There was no reasoning with drunks.

"The Gang of Four are probably delirious from the heavy intake of alcohol," Arisi said to Kuychi, "causing them to holler and yell, but what they were hollering and yelling about is the concern. Are they seeing things that none of us can? Or..." he paused, "Never mind, it's probably nothing."

On the north side of the village, four young men, all drinking buddies, referred to by other villagers as "The Gang of Four," Kichka, Manqu, Waywa, and Yanamayu, were regulars in the thicket of trees. The lads were all in their mid-teens, single, and preferred the company of men, an odd habit noticed by the other villagers, but seldom discussed publicly. They were already drunk, overconsuming home-brewed potato alcohol, called Killa k'anchay, nearly oblivious to the daylight as it disappeared on the western horizon.

The four young men laughed, teased, and joked with one another, which sounded more like mindless babbling, when one of them glanced through the thicket trees, seeing what he thought to be a fire. Yanamayu wobbled to his feet and blinked several times, trying to get his eyes to focus. Imagining he saw tall blazing flames in the trees, Yanamayu yelled awkwardly, "F-f-f-f-fire! F-f-f-fire! Fi-i-i-i-i-i-re!"

Taking a few seconds for an alarming cry to sink in, the other three men staggered and stumbled to their feet as quickly as they were able. Mentally, they were in no condition to make a reasonable assessment of Yanamayu's claim, reacting purely out of fear. The hysteria was instant. None of the four men could decide what to do. They all chose to run in poorly chosen directions in the same instance, slamming into each other and falling back down to where they'd been sitting moments before.

The four men laughed at the craziness for a split second before remembering they were in danger. Looking through the thicket, they saw enormous "flames," becoming brighter and ever closer. Kichka began hollering, while Manqu yelled, and both Waywa and Yanamayu screamed.

As the 'flames' ascended above the trees, all four drunken men gasped and looked wide-eyed in shock and disbelief. Drinking had distorted what they were seeing. There were no flames, no fire. It was something out of their world! Orange lights showed down on them from an enormous black triangular-shaped object in the air, just above the treetops and moving overhead. The men were momentarily frozen. Nothing seemed quite right to them, particularly what they were seeing!

As the massive object moved over them, Kichka suddenly yelled out, "What is it?"

Then Manqu panicked and cried out, "Let's go!"

Waywa yelled, "NOW!" as he blindly turned to run and immediately hit the trunk of a large tree with his total weight, falling to the ground unconscious. Seeing Waywa fall, Kichka stopped with the thought of helping his pal, but decided to save himself as he looked up at the object passing overhead. He stumbled forward again, never entirely coordinating his legs to run.

Yanamayu and Manqu were incapacitated. They attempted to run but kept falling over. They used their arms in a futile attempt to balance and steady themselves but were exhausted and fell to the ground, finally giving up.

Meanwhile, Kuychi and Arisi had decided to disregard the racket, but a woman screamed from another direction just then. Then more people were yelling. The sounds were coming from everywhere in the village.

The couple scrambled out of bed, hurriedly pulled on their clothes, and dashed outside. Despite the darkness, all the villagers were outside their houses yelling, screaming, shouting, and pointing up at the sky. There were orange lights overhead, getting everyone's attention.

The excitement and screaming of children in other parts of Sonqollaqta brought the 'thing' to the villagers' attention. Something unusual was in progress.

There were shouts of all kinds,

"Lights are shining down!"

"Wow, look in the sky!"

"Look at the columns of light."

"Look in the sky!"

"Something strange is in the sky!"

"Look up!"

"What is that?"

"Come see this strange thing!"

"Small light globes are moving through the village!"

Arisi and Kuychi ran out of their house to investigate the commotion for themselves.

Both were wonderstruck when they saw orange lights moving overhead; lights shining down on the village as they passed over. The villagers' mouths hung open as they stared at the black 'thing', immediately noticing an orange circular light at each corner and a much larger one in the middle of the enormous black triangle, creating a daylight effect as it moved over the village. The object itself was black like the night, and shiny.

The size of the thing, Arisi thought to himself, is *half the length of the scattered houses of the village and moves slowly and silently like a gigantic condor gliding in the sky.*

The village suddenly darkened again as the lights moved up the mountainside above the settlement. The curiosity of many of the inhabitants immediately prompted them to follow, determined to see where the thing was going. A few, more hesitant, stood stationary and watched the orange lights, as they were the only means of seeing where the object was going.

Most of the village inhabitants had become spectators to a once-in-a-lifetime event they hadn't even paid to watch. All the spectators proceeded on a well-used dirt path up the mountain slope in clusters of different sizes—families, friends, or couples.

From indications, the thing in the sky was on a course to the lake in the higher montane grassland, less than an hour away. Whether it would stop at the lake was anyone's guess. But it didn't contain the enthusiasm urging the villagers on.

The lights showed the object moving slowly on an ascending angle parallel with the terrain, continuing to pass over the landscape that plateaued where the grassland started, and coming to a hover.

From what the villagers could tell from a distance, the flying thing was over the lake.

"It's at the lake!' Arisi shouted excitedly. He heard several other people saying almost the same thing simultaneously,

"It stopped at the lake."

"The lake!"

"It stopped at the lake!"

It's at the lake!"

It stopped at the lake!" The words echoed out into the otherwise silent night. The enthusiasm grew, and the villagers hurried along faster, which saw some start to fall behind.

With the first few villagers, Kuychi and Arisi crossed over the pass. The string of villagers had gotten longer as some slowed their pace; some walked steadily; still, others stopped temporarily to catch their breath. However, none of them returned to Sonqollaqta. Regardless, this experience would be something they could talk about for the rest of their lives.

The villagers began to gather near the east shoreline of the lake and watched excitedly for a considerable length of time as the triangular object silently hovered over the water.

At the same time, the number of villagers continued to grow as more and more trickled in. There were only a few low whispers; others were silent, awestruck, and staring at the mysterious thing hanging in the air.

Suddenly, the object in the sky began moving away from the lake's center to the shore on the villager's left. The excitement and noise among the villagers increased, as they anticipated something more exciting was about to happen; but, once the black triangle was over the land, it stopped again.

The orange lights continued illuminating the shoreline and adjacent land beneath the triangular object. Finally, the gigantic light in the middle began to exhibit particle waves in three columns of sparkling light, and instantly, three human-like forms appeared standing next to each other on the ground.

A short distance away from the Sonqollaqta villagers stood beings from a different world and beyond any of the notions these Quechuans' may have of reality, and their ideas of how humans look. Yet, as Arisi saw them, the aliens looked very similar: Slender, with their limbs proportional to overall height. They all had six fingers and six toes. Their heads were bald and perfectly round on top. All had almond-shaped, blue eyes, the same longish noses, sizeable lower lips but hardly an upper lip, pointed chins, translucent brownish-red skin. They were naked from the waist up, their perfectly spherical breasts exposed, and wore skin-tight garments on the lower half of their bodies.

These beings were shockingly unfamiliar to the villagers of Sonqollaqta. Never in their wildest imagination could they have created such beings. All the strangeness sent a gigantic emotional shock wave through the crowd that temporarily stunned them, their emotions mixed. Some stood motionless in absolute awe, stunned, shocked by the partial nudity, Still, others were surprised, fearful, suspicious. Some stared silently in disbelief. Some shouted, "Pagla (bald)!" Some were excited, impressed, and amazed. Finally, others were eager to understand what was beyond their immediate comprehension.

Arisi and Kuychi, like the others, looked at each other with wonderment written across their faces. But immediately, Arisi, surprising himself, said to Kuychi, "Ch'usaq Pacha (celestial gods)!"

A myriad of questions arose among the spectators:

Who are they?

Are these the Ch'usaq Pacha?

From where did these beings come?

What do these shuckuna (strangers) want of us?

Do the Ch'usaq Pacha look like this?

Why are they here?

Now what?

What is there to learn from these beings?

Have they come to tell us something?

Do other worlds exist?

Who will believe us when we tell them?

Standing at the edge of the villagers closest to the Ch'usaq Pacha, Arisi unexpectedly began walking toward them with Kuychi in tow, leaving the crowd of villagers behind. Kuychi hesitated until he looked at her, then all her resistance melted.

"We're moved by a power other than our own!" Arisi said to Kuychi, reflecting a momentary surge of uncertainty in the couple.

"Are you sure this is a good idea?" Kuychi questioned suspiciously. These feelings were short-lived. An unexpected wave of peace washed over them as they approached these Gods from who-knows-where.

Kuychi was suspicious while Arisi wondered, *what is the purpose of this unbelievable encounter? How am I going to talk with these Ch'usaq Pacha? They probably don't speak my language, and I am sure I don't communicate in theirs."*

Unexpectedly came a telepathic reply. *We need no words, only pure thought which will pass between us. We can 'tune in' to the neuroreceptors of other beings. No matter the language we speak, you will 'hear' your language. Between ourselves, we use telepathy to communicate. The use of audible language is minimal.*

Amazed at what he heard, Arisi stared at the faces of all three beings to determine which one had answered him as he had seen no lip movement from any of them. He could not. He did, however, understand he would be able to talk comfortably with these strangers. Realizing he could talk to them did have a calming effect on him.

The alien being in the middle raised her hand. *I am Xepe.* Her lips didn't move.

The one to the right of Xepe raised her hand. *I am Xoa.* Again, no lip movement. The one to the left of Xepe raised her hand, and *I am Xetu.*

Then Arisi blurted out, "Are you the sacred Ch'usaq Pacha who our ancestors have talked about for many, many, many moons?"

We come from a different world. We are your ancestors from the very distant past and your future. You live in a dimension where events are often ordered from the past through the present into the future. We can access different timelines. So, we can visit your blue planet in what you call the past, present, or future. We know what is happening in your world when we tune in to the energy frequencies here. One easy way to show you this is simply saying you knew we were coming.

Kuychi looked at Arisi, wondering *how* she or he would *know?*

Arisi's unanticipated response surprised his wife and all the villagers.

A shaman in Paucartambo told me the village would have an unexpected visit from strangers, Arisi answered by thought projection, *but I had no idea it would be from the stars! All the villagers know I travel down the eastern slope to lower elevations from time to time to trade papas and wool for articles hard to make or obtain at our altitude. However, they did not know I consulted with a shaman in the lowlands for* divination *purposes on my last trip. So, I had a premonition that something unusual would occur and wanted to see if he could find out more about it.*

Kuychi was amazed that the Ch'usaq Pacha knew of Arisi's visit with a shaman in the lowlands.

But the present moment held a different interest for Aris. He wondered, *Am I going to embarrass myself in front of my wife? I'm feeling myself getting hard staring at the naked bodies of these women with perfectly shaped breasts!*

To save himself, Arisi said aloud, forgetting the telepathic nature of their conversation in a moment of erotic excitement, "You three are women!"

*We are a race of neither women nor men. Each is male **and** female and has the sex organs of both sexes. All species on our planet, including plants and animals, are male AND female.*

*"Each of you is male **and** female!" Arisi exclaimed, in shock.*

Although surprised at the dual sexual nature of their bodies, which was beyond his comprehension, Arisi was open to knowing more, but not at that moment. Instead, Arisi shifted to a question he'd intended to ask earlier before getting aroused by their partial nudity, "Where is your home in the sky?"

Xepe pointed behind Arisi, who followed the angle of this celestial God's extended arm and turned to see where it pointed. *The brightest star visible, Chukichinchay* (Sirius*)!* he thought, then shouted out loud to his wife, "Kuychi, they are from Chukichinchay! Chukichinchay!" A surge of excitement engulfed Arisi. "You know, the sparkling multi-colored head of the rainbow serpent, Mach'acuray, in the night sky."

Kuychi blinked her eyes in surprise and looked at him curiously. "I remember the name from our conversation one night," she confessed, "when you were pointing to the stars, but no more than that. You know much more about the stars and Quechuan stargazing as it relates to farming than I care to know."

The confirmation came from the visitors. *Yes, we are from Chukichinchay. Yet I must say distance impairs observation. The farther one is from the focus of attention; the fewer details are visible. So, you call our world Chukichinchay. It is not just one star but three stars, each having at least one planet orbiting it with human life.*

We are from Ashkera, the brightest star and the only one of the three stars you see with the naked eyes. You call it Chukichinchay. Without getting too involved, the other two stars are Thula (Sirius

B) and Emerya (Sirius C). Each star has at least one planet orbiting it that has human life on it.

Arisi raised his eyebrows in surprise and amazement at what was being expressed.

I will draw it on the ground for you.

The Xepe knelt and, with the side of his hand, scraped the pebbles and rocks aside in an area big enough to draw what she intended on the flat surface of the ground exposed.

Arisi bent over at the waist to focus his attention directly on what Xepe was doing, but his eyes were drawn to the Xepe's hand, a soft brownish-red smooth skin with six fingers and thumb. He looked at the palm of his left hand for comparison and was amazed that his hand was small in contrast.

Knowing the Quechuan's thoughts, Xepe looked up at him. Arisi, staring into the blue eyes of this God, was captivated, losing his bearing briefly. Xepe looked down again, redirecting Arisi's attention to the ground. The extraterrestrial poked a depression in the soil with a slender forefinger and drew three concentric circles around it, each larger.

This largest circle is the outer orbit of a white dwarf star, Thula, which you cannot see from your planet. Xepe put a stone on the circle. *The next smaller is the trajectory of a blue-green giant star, Ashkera, you see in your night sky and call Chukichinchay.* He grabbed a much larger stone and put it on that circle. *The center point of both circles is a burnt-out black dwarf star (Emerya).* Quickly finding a small stone, Xepe placed it in the dead center of the circles. Then she placed another pebble close to Ashkera. *This last stone represents our home planet Kashta, which orbits Ashkera. It is one of six planets orbiting Ashkera and is the second planet from Ashkera.*

Very interesting. Thank you for showing me, Xepe. Arisi responded as he and the celestial being stood upright, then he added, *I have a clear understanding of what you said and will make sure this correction is in Quechua folklore. Like us, it* makes *more sense* than living on stars, but planets that go around stars!

You understand correctly, Xepe's answer sounded in Arisi's head.

Knowing who was answering his questions, Arisi asked Xepe, "How far away is Chukichinchay?"

Xepe didn't answer but turned to Xoa. She replied instead, *A distance you probably cannot imagine, 8.6 lightyears. Expressed in your watas (years), it is a seventy-two quadrillion wata journey. However, the travel time is affected by the speed of travel. In our case, we used a velocity faster than light, a fragmentation process whereby matter is reduced to the absolute smallest size, approaching non-existence. A moment when movement from one point to another is inconceivably fast. That is, one trillionth of a nanosecond per one light-year of distance. For you, it means INSTANTLY. Disappear there and reappear here and reassembled to original size.*

The last bit of information was incomprehensible to the Quechuan. *I didn't get it all, but I understand the 'disappear there and reappear here' idea*, the young man commented, *our people call it magic.*

Why have you come here, an unbelievable distance from your home? Arisi wanted to know.

We have colonized planets in distant galaxies, as we have in your Mayu, and this is not our first time coming to your world, as I have said before. We've traveled in our starship and colonized different parts of your planet as far back in time as several thousand watas earlier. Atlantis, on the north edge of a body of water called the Black Sea, became a highly organized and complex society eventually destroyed by an upheaval in the earth's crust. There is another place not too far from here, in the tropical lowlands, that we colonized. Of course, there are other places on your planet too.

Our *objective is to spread peace and change for the better.* The telepathic voice further stated, *we have come bearing a gift to help improve your lives. I mean a more peaceful and loving existence and greater appreciation for life.*

What sort of gift could that be? Arisi mused. *Maybe a new tool for cultivating the soil? Perhaps a new way to build houses? Maybe a new plant or seed for us to sow? Perhaps a new way to organize our lives.*

None of those, the voice said, interrupting his thoughts, *more valuable to life than any of those possibilities.*

What is it? Arisi begged, looking at his wife, who shrugged her shoulders, not knowing.

Xepe turned her back to Arisi and stood motionless while another sparkling of particle waves in the orange light became visible to everyone watching. Almost instantly, another celestial being materialized holding something Arisi could not see from his position, nor could Kuychi from hers, nor any of the villagers standing a distance away. Xepe turned back around, facing Arisi and Kuychi, and the fourth God stepped forward in line with the other three.

I am Xona.

"Look, Arisi, she's holding a baby!" Kuychi exclaimed loudly.

"This can't be the gift," Arisi protested, "A baby?"

Xona, the baby in her hands, stepped forward to Kuychi and Arisi and extended the baby to them. Then, pulling a shawl off, Kuychi's nurturing instinct took over. She took the baby and wrapped it in her cloak. "Look, Arisi," she said excitedly, "What a beautiful boy with those captivating blue eyes. Just the boy I've wanted! I'll take him."

Stone-deaf to his wife's decision, Arisi was flustered, focused on several questions, which caused him to forget he was communicating by thought alone. Instead, he blurted out loud—

"What are we to do with this child? Who's going to be responsible for his life? Does it need special food? Where is..........." and incoming telepathic message interrupted him.

Unlike the explorers that roam your planet who have decimated indigenous peoples they've contacted with disease, damaging economies, destroying political structures, and forcing acceptance of new ideologies, we are explorers of the Universe bringing to you a gift: A human baby, a boy, who is to be raised as one of your own, making this contact the entry point into the reincarnation cycle on this planet for the spirit of this boy.

This child from Chukichinchay, however, is not the first of his kind as the Ch'usaq Pacha have made hundreds of such 'starseed drops' on what we call the Blue Planet in a manner so clever and indirect as to delicately influence the spiritual development of its inhabitants.

'Drops' are a means the Ch'usaq Pacha use to comply with the fundamental law in the galaxy: Non-interference. The mandate deals primarily with interaction between spacefaring civilizations and non-spacefaring, stating the former should not interfere in the latter's development without adequate cause.

"Ok, but who in the village is to raise this baby? Attend to his needs?" Arisi asked again aloud, his obsession with the care of the child having totally dismissed what Xona had transmitted.

Then Xeta, standing to the left of Xepe, stepped forward, and by telepathy, asked, *Are you two without a child?*

Amazed this celestial being knew they had no children, Kuychi answered with her thoughts, *Arisi and I have no child.* Then she looked at Arisi with a smile, cradling the child in her arms. She lovingly kissed the baby on the forehead. "He's mine now!" she added out loud with a broad smile.

Perfect, Xona replied, *Raise this baby as your own. His genetic make-up is almost identical to yours. He is heterosexual, although I, an androgenous being, gave birth to him. Teach him what he needs to know as you would any child who must learn your culture to survive. He will return your kindness many times over and affect many who come to know him and know of him. He will have abilities beyond what you can imagine.*

"We are honored," Kuychi said in her humblest voice and bowing her head.

All of you are now part of our family. You are welcome any time you wish to drop in, Arisi replied with his thoughts.

Thank you for your kindness, an anonymous voice said, adding, *your words carry the spirit of our home planet. If there is to be another time, you will see us four. Thank you for opening your hearts and opening your lives to the undreamed of possibilities.*

Arisi gently took the baby into his arms and turned to the gathering of villagers. Then, extending the baby over his head, he yells, "Our gift from Ch'usaq Pacha!"

The villagers began cheering and shouting words of approval. Some jumped up and down. Some hugged each other. Others were laughing joyfully, while still others shed tears of joy.

Kuychi turned to the aliens, placing the palms of her hands together, bowed, and thought to the aliens, *Arisi, I, and our people can never thank you enough.* The three aliens lowered their heads as a gesture of acceptance, as tears streamed down Kuychi's cheeks.

As a final telepathic transmission, the voice said, *we hope your world can change to become like ours. This gift is another start in that direction. On our planet, there is no greed, no hatred, no inequality, no injustice, no male, no female, no ruler, or servant, no greater, no lesser.* Instead, *we all support peaceful co-existence, emphasizing the well-being of all. We depart, having enjoyed our brief visit.*

Kuychi grabbed Arisi's shoulder as a wave of sadness suddenly intruded upon her happiness. She said, "Arisi, they are leaving, and I hate to see them go." He gave the baby to her, turned to the gathering of villagers, and shouted, "You have heard their words, and now the Ch'usaq Pacha leave us! Let us show them a warm leaving."

To the surprise of the celestial beings, the villagers rushed down to touch the Gods from the planet Kashta in the Chukichinchay star system, knowing they would never see them again but never forget them.

As the villagers swarmed around the Xepe, Xoa, Xoni, Xeta, Kuychi, Arisi, and the baby, touching each of them as a blessing to their lives, Arisi looked at Kuychi, smiled, and said, "Ch'askawani (Star Eyes)."

"Perfect, my love, perfect name for our son," she responded enthusiastically, then cast a warm gaze and smiled upon the baby.

"And this spot, this beautiful lake, may it be known as the place of an Imananopis llapan kamakanqan," Arisi announced.

Again, Kuychi smiled and nodded in agreement.

Then, unexpectedly she saw it: the telltale sign, the mark. The baby's left hand had five fingers and a thumb. "Arisi!" she called to get his attention. "Look at the baby's left hand."

Arisi widened his eyes and lifted his eyebrows in an expression of surprise at what he saw, but said nothing, knowing, like Kuychi, it was the one visible sign of the little one's origin.

Kuychi thought to herself, *the baby's hand is evidence of his birth in the Stars, which would require an unavoidable explanation at some point in the years to come.*

The Ch'usaq Pacha delivered, unbeknownst to the villagers receiving him, a spiritually upgraded being veiled as an innocent baby. Neither did any of them have the vaguest notion of the seismic force that would shake their lives, nor did they know when, why or how it would happen.

2

Kuychi and Arisi were considered courageous for talking with the Celestial Gods on behalf of the village. Many villagers considered them heroes. This change in status brought on many other changes, both expected and unexpected, in their relationships with the other villagers. So did the presence of baby Ch'askawani. The quiet and private life of Kuychi and Arisi's household suddenly took on the appearance of a popular spot, busy and public.

Villagers were frequent visitors, bestowing gifts on the child whom all considered sacred. Then, unexpectedly, many came seeking counsel on matters of all kinds. Finally, the couple concluded it was simply their association with the child.

In addition to the domestic responsibilities and duties of having a child, the community added obligations. Kuychi and Arisi took on these new obligations to their lives with humility, as an honor bestowed upon them.

Arisi was appointed an "elder" of the village by the unanimous vote of all the villagers. Shortly after that, he became a trader for the entire settlement in any negotiations of large volumes of papas (potatoes) that the villagers wished to trade with the lowlanders in exchange for other desired goods.

An additional obligation was to take Ch'askawani, who seemed like any other child his age, to the community gatherings that began to take place once a month. The townspeople considered the little child sacred, believing him to be their good fortune. Group prayers for a good crop yield were conducted, while others were more personal, for the sick, the elderly, and the infirmed.

The result of these ongoing gatherings was that many of the elderly were revived, the infirmed rejuvenated, the sick, healed, whether by the invisible power of the villagers' collective thoughts, or by their belief in the abilities of the sacred child.

As more visitors saw the baby boy close-up, more saw the six digits on his left hand, the striking visual connection with the Ch'usaq Pacha that only those present the night of contact had seen for themselves. Ch'askawani's hand was the sign of His Divinity, a constant reminder of his sky-born status and the reverence accompanying that status. This awareness solidified respect for the boy throughout Sonqollaqta.

The villagers' confirmation of the little boy's powerful intervention during the prayer gatherings was his tendency to raise his "God hand" when the group spoke a person's name.

By the age of three, the boy spoke Quechua and showed a great memory, knowing the names of all the villagers who visited him, which showed he was intelligent.

Arisi and Kuychi never stopped showering Ch'askawani with their love and praise. But, unbeknownst to the couple, their resolute devotion to the child had transformed their attitude toward everyone else in the settlement.

A noticeable change in the actions of Arisi and Kuychi was first brought to Kuychi's attention one day by a widow named Urma, who lived alone in a small house since the death of her husband. She was short, rotunda, wore a bright yellow sweater and black shirt with a colorful hem. She had a warm and disarming personality.

Urma had come to visit one afternoon, along with several other village women, to pay their respects to Ch'askawani. While other women sat seeking advice from the sacred boy, Urma pulled Kuychi aside, "It's been five years since Ch'askawani came into our lives. Whatever change has come about in your interaction with him it has rubbed off on your way of dealing with others. Your name is on the lips of many in the village lately."

"That's so sweet of you to say, Urma," Kuychi replied humbly and respectfully.

"I appreciate you allowing us to participate in Ch'askawani's life. What a blessing!" Urma added appreciatively.

"Urma, I am deeply grateful for your comments," Kuychi admitted, adding, "Just the other day, Arisi and I were talking about this very thing. Arisi was telling me about a comment Ch'askawani had made to him. The boy said, 'I have heard people call me 'the sacred one' and as a result show me respect and reverence. What they need to realize is the deeper meaning behind their thoughts. The more something or someone is valued and seen as sacred, the more re-spect, admiration, and reverence flows **through those doing the viewing**. What one experiences is themselves. It's what appears in the eyes of the beholder. The one perceiving another is the one projecting those qualities onto another. The perspective used to view the world reflects the viewer, not the world; only the viewer's world. So, the more one sees another as sacred, the more sacred the viewer becomes. The view and the viewer are not separate issues.' Ch'askawani's words were very enlightening, I thought," Kuychi concluded.

"So," Urma ventured, "to see everyone as valuable and consider them sacred is to hold a view that is itself sacred!"

"Exactly, Urma!"

"Maybe it's time that ideas like this have a broader airing," Urma offered. "Ch'askawani must have been brought by the Ch'asuq Pacha to change our lives. You and Arisi can help bring this about. Our gatherings can be of even greater benefit than just healing our bodies. Our minds need healing too."

The conversation ended with Kuychi saying, "Urma, that's an excellent idea. I will talk with Arisi and Ch'askawani."

Kuychi and Urma's attention returned to the scared boy, still "holding court." Then, Kuychi and Urma overheard one of the quests, Huayta, who was younger, taller, and more robust than Urma, and wore a black umbrella hat, pink sweater, and dark blue shirt, ask, "Most precious Ch'askawani, my mother is very old. She is sick, and the condition worsens. I am concerned she may die. But she tells me she does not want to go yet."

"Trust that her power is in her will to live," was the boy's only answer.

The next day Arisi and Ch'askawani were sitting outside near the front of the house when Arisi offered the boy an invitation, "Would you like to come with me down the slope to Paucartambo? I have wool I promised to trade for one of the other villagers. We will be back in three days."

"Oh yes, Arisi! I want to go!" The sacred youngster replied, instantly excited at the prospect.

"Good, we leave in a little while. I need to load wool on a llama, then we'll go."

Ch'askawani's unfamiliar spiritual perspective, already developed by age five, was brought home one day to Kuychi, when she lovingly said to him as they sat outside their house on camelid hides at mid-day, "It is an honor to be your mama, Ch'askawani."

There was no way for him to know whether she was expressing undying affection, or expressing an unfulfilled need for attention. In either case, his response surprised her.

"I am not your child. I am the Divine longing to know itself, as are you. I do not say this to crush you, but to crush the idea of what you think I am and you are," Ch'askawani said slowly and softly. "We are all expressions of the One Divinity that I am, and you are, and everyone else is. I call you Mama, but I want you to know what is real to me, not the ideas you believe are real."

Kuychi sat silent. She had not chosen to be quiet; but was speechless. Then, moments later, she thought, *A mouthful from such a small boy.* Somewhat unnerved, Kuychi took several moments digging through her conditioning to uncover the gem revealed in her son's words.

"You need not fear," the boy added, "You can never lose yourself. You can only lose..."

"...Ah, only the ideas I have of myself and anyone else," Kuychi interrupted. Then she broke out in a loud belly laugh and, with a spark of genius, said, "Nuqa-Qamta" (me-you).

Ch'askawani smiled broadly and replied, "Qamta-Nuqa" (you-me).

Kuychi repeated herself, "Nuqa-Qamta. Nuqa-Qamta. Nuqa-Qamta."

The boy repeated his response three times, "Qamta-Nuqa. Qamta-Nuqa. Qamta-Nuqa."

Both laughed uproariously and hugged each other, unintentionally creating nicknames for each other in a moment of insight for Kuychi; nicknames that would be with them for the rest of their lives. She would occasionally be called Me-You by him, and Ch'askawani, You-Me by her. As profound and remarkable as their warm, loving relationship was, the atmosphere of openness it created enabled them to experience each moment as fresh and new. Seeing things anew is a spiritual adventure, whereas seeing them the same is tradition.

"You-me, I am so happy you are in my life and equally happy I am in yours," Ch'askawani admitted, leaning toward her and hugging her, adding, "You are open to a new world, which means a new you. Change is important. In the Stars, they say, "Change is endlessness experiencing itself."

"You are so wise, little one," Kuychi acknowledged. "You will teach me much in our time together."

"As long as you are willing to learn, Mama. Remember, as profound as a warm, loving relationship is, the expansion of the minds of both is equally important. When things are viewed the same, monotony sets in and with it, a loss of inspiration, a lack of enthusiasm, a replacement of caring with carelessness."

Kuychi nodded. She understood.

Much later, Arisi returned from cultivating papas in one of his fields and heard the exchange of nicknames for the first time. "So, what is this change in names I am hearing?" Arisi, with a disarming smile, inquired of Kuychi.

Instantly she began chuckling, then commented, "I've learned if I hold tightly to the ideas of who I am like Kuychi, mama, wife, woman, I miss acknowledging the Divine I am, the Divine One who exists as all. The nickname 'Me-You,' which came to me in a flash of insight expressed childishly, is a simple way of releasing all these ideas, these identities, enabling nuna (consciousness) to focus on 'What Is' while living in this world.

"I am not saying what you perceive doesn't exist. It is because you perceive me as your wife that I exist **for you** as your wife."

Arisi hugged Kuychi, then kissed her. "I loved it. You are becoming wise, my love. Unfortunately, wisdom is not understood by the ignorant," he offered.

"Maybe so," she replied, lovingly, "But if I, who has been ignorant, can begin to perceive wisdom in what is said, might there be a starting point for others as well? And, as more and more of our people see it this way, will it not affect all of us? And our thinking as well?

"Yes, you are right!" were the words Arisi mustered up, validating her comments.

It seemed like, as soon as Arisi and Ch'askawani departed Sonqollaqta on their trip down the eastern slope, they were back. Three days had passed. Unexpected things had happened.

Within sight of the village, Arisi had noticed the fields below the settlement were empty, unusual for that time of year when the papas needed cultivating; but no one was in the area. *Odd*, he thought and wondered why. Ch'askawani knew why. Yet neither of them said anything.

The two travelers entered the lower side of the village, Arisi walking and Ch'askawani joyfully riding the llama. Nearing their house, they saw Kuychi returning from a nearby mountain stream with water, approaching too. Their paths converged near the front of the house.

Kuychi smiled and spoke first. "So happy to see you two. Not so surprising, Miski died the afternoon you left for Paucartambo. Relatives have already dug a grave and placed her body outside the house today on skins, in preparation for burial. We can go anytime you want to pay our respects to Huayta, Kusi, and other relatives before the funeral later today.

"Do you and Ch'askawani want to go immediately?" Arisi asked, "If that is so, I can follow shortly. I need to remove the cargo frame from the llama and release it into the corral."

"I prefer we go together," Kuychi quickly replied.

"As you wish," Arisi said, turning toward the corral and pulling on the rope bridle to get the llama's attention. The corral was a short distance.

When the three got close to Huayta's house, they saw the large gathering of mourners, some weeping, others in whispered conversation, still others with heads bowed in silence.

The villagers who noticed their approach stepped aside, clearing the way for them to see Miski's body laid out on camelid skins adorned with flowers on her chest and all around the body.

The scene showed the sorrow of many. Huayta, viewed from the back, was on her knees and bent over her mother's body.

Kuychi and Arisi stopped a few steps away while young Ch'askawani stepped forward alongside the bereaved Huayta. He bent down and gently put his hand on her shoulder. Immediately tears formed in his eyes, feeling the woman's sorrow. Huayta turned, hugged him tightly, and began to cry loudly. Ch'askawani held her quietly until her weeping subsided.

Then, she pulled back slightly to face the boy and spoke through her sobbing, "Miski was a wonderful mother and wonderful person. I will miss her greatly. Her loss is like tearing out a piece of me. I had hoped, Precious One, you might be able to save her, but that was not to be."

Without another word, this remarkable boy, who had shown his great wisdom but not his healing might, in full view of everyone, turned and faced the dead body. He laid his left hand on the body and began staring straight ahead.

Silence came over the mourners as they watched him with keen interest. Ch'askawani could hear their thoughts.

What will he do?

No one can bring the dead back to life.

What can he do?

The boy will do something miraculous!

No one can bring back the dead.

Then he heard Huayta's special prayer,

Please, oh precious Ch'askawani, *bring my sweet* mama *back to* her body and to me. *Please know we* love *you, mama, and want* you *back unless it is your wish to go.*

Kuychi and Arisi stood silently but with anticipation. Arisi thought, *This boy is beyond what these people can imagine, and what he will do, I am sure, will shock even me.* Then, he took a deep breath, looked at his wife, and said, "I am so excited to see what happens."

Kuychi smiled back at him. They knew this was a telling moment for the young boy who was well beyond his years in both wisdom and healing ability.

Ch'askawani, having psychic powers, knew the departed spirit was still near the body, even though the body was cold to his touch. He knew because, with his 'faraway face,' he was staring at the spirit standing on the other side of the body, staring back at him! Only he could see it. So, he spoke to it telepathically, *Is it your* genuine *desire to leave the body?*

I didn't want to leave, but my will was fading. I had no realization of how much I was loved and by so many until this moment, the spirit replied.

Ch'askawani spoke telepathically again, *Now is your opportunity to return to the body. The cold has stopped the body from starting to decay, and it has no foul odor yet. However, sooner than later, the process will begin and an opportunity to return to the body will be lost.*

The spirit, unmoved and still staring at Ch'askawani, finally responded, *I do not wish to go now. I became unsure whether I could maintain that heavy body after knowing what it feels like without it. But you have helped me see I can overcome anything by my will. So, I am ready to return now.*

I want you to lay in the body and do as I say, he instructed.

Ch'askawani quietly watched the spirit's movement as it laid down in the body.

Many more moments passed in silence and without any noticeable action. The only movement detected by the crowd was the boy's eyes moving from staring straight ahead to looking down at the Miski's body, which caused several to doubt whether anything would happen.

Suddenly Ch'askawani stood up and stepped back. Then he commanded in a soft but firm voice, "Open your eyes and stand up! There was a sudden convulsive effort to breathe by Miski's body. The old woman opened her eyes and slowly got up. Seeing the boy standing in front of her, she smiled and quietly said, "Thank you."

Huayta screamed in ecstasy as she ran to her mother and embraced her tightly as tears streamed down her face, "Mama! Mama! You are back with us. I can't believe it!"

Then Arisi added a cheer, "Ch'askawani brought Miski back from the dead!"

There was a complete change in the mood of those gathered. Some began cheering joyfully, one of many emotions expressed simultaneously.

For the townspeople, the abrupt transformation was unbelievable. Traditional thought patterns shifted instantly for some. What was before inconceivable, was now knowable.

Direct experience had just overrun entrenched traditional Quechuan ideas about life. The experience erased several thought files, replacing them with new ones. Tremendously powerful mental and emotional disturbances were occurring, a shock wave of energy. Some accepted the changes occurring in their thinking; some were dubious; still others resisted what they had seen with their own eyes.

As the villagers began to quiet down, they heard a shout, and it hushed the crowd: "Ch'askawani, what did you do?

What was asked was the singular question in the minds of many that would answer their lingering curiosity and hopefully remove the shroud of mystery yet hanging over Miski's unforeseen rise from the dead. Sudden change can beget great wonder and be unsettling too. Many villagers wanted to know how it happened.

But Ch'askawani had a different take on the situation, thinking to himself, *In the face of significant change, people's egos do not give up their 'dead' quickly! So, he* chose to allow Miski to tell her experience, *"Miski, will you explain what happened to you, or, at least, what you learned from it?"*

Ch'askawani's strategy made the villagers realize they were even more curious than they first knew.

Miski broke free from her daughter's arms and took a couple of steps into the space created by where she had been laying. She looked around at the many familiar faces staring back at her, cleared her throat, and began, "One of the first things I learned right away when I stopped breathing and separated from my body seemed so obvious: I was not the body. Why? Because I was separate from it and viewed it from beyond it. Then I thought, I am alive and not in the body. Instantly, I realized the body dies, but I don't.

"Out-of-body, I was in a state where I could hear everything going on around me. I listened to my daughter and granddaughter weeping and saw them draped over the body and felt their loss.

But they could not see and hear me right beside them, trying to console them. And that is the way it was when I went to the houses of others of you. I could see you and hear you, but you could not hear or see me; but I was there. For example, yesterday morning, I went to Atoc and Quasi's house. Atoc was gone, and Quasi was home alone. I watched her preparing a red dye. She happened to move too quickly and dropped a ceramic pot she was holding, and it broke, hitting the ground. Am I right, Quasi?"

"Oh, my word, yes! Unbelievable! I thought no one would know!" was the reply shouted back.

"So, in those three days, no one could see me or hear me out-of-body except Ch'askawani, as I found out today, which tells me this Precious One lives in both states at the same time.

"I began to think being dead and out-of-body was like being a Pacha (a God)!

"I was amazed I was able to move by thought alone. Think about that for a moment. I had no physical body to move around, which requires my energy! When I went to Atoc and Quasi's house and others I visited, I would think about who I wanted to see, picture their house, and instantly I was there." Miski laughed, "I moved by thought alone, as odd as it may sound. Even hearing me say it sounds odd, and I experienced it!"

There was laughter from among the villagers. Then someone yelled, "You mean you could touch us, and we wouldn't feel you doing it?"

"Yes, that surprised me too. I was still alive. I was real, but without a body to touch with. I was just an energy touching you.

"What amazes me as much as anything was, **I didn't need anything**! No food. No sleep. Nothing. If that isn't paradise, I don't know what is!"

"Why did you come back then?" another voice called out.

"Before I dropped my body, I had no desire to leave. After leaving my body and knowing I was still alive, I wasn't sure I wanted to get back into this heavy body, which is like wearing ten ponchos at the same time. But I could hear everyone's thoughts of me, and to hear your love for me expressed. I wanted to share more time with all of you. Love is a special gift. Other than that, I can't say why I came back. Maybe I was meant to share my experience with all of you. Perhaps it is my gift to you for all the love you have given me.

"Life is different than we think. Think about that! We just are. We are in a constant state of existence. We don't die. We may leave a body when it's worn out like an old shirt or old pair of pants, and get another to start all over again." Miski took a deep breath, "Well, that's my story, and I am sticking to it."

Miski turned and looked at Ch'askawani, wondering if there was anything else he wanted from her.

"Now, Miski, can you tell everyone here what I did that brought you back to your body?" this mysterious young boy asked.

"Yes, I was asked if I wanted to stay or to go." Miski said, "Ch'askawani told me I had so much time before the body would start to decay. It was my decision. Feeling the love of many was an energy pulling me back into this life. So, when I decided to return, he asked me to lay back down in my body and the rest of his instructions were all heard.

"If there is a mystery here, it's Ch'askawani, his ability to be in two worlds—the here and the hereafter—at the same time. To me, that is the Divine miracle that happened. Coming and going is just an individual decision. That was the only thing this boy helped me see. He helped me realize my power was always in my hands, now and forever, to experience as **I choose**. That was the most important thing. I was able to experience what it is like to see this world from a different point of view. Then, with Ch'askawani's extraordinary ability to communicate with the other side, I was able to come back with a new awareness and share that point of view.

Miski lifted both her arms, indicating that was all she had to say.

"Thank you, Beloved Miski. I only want to add, we all gain a new awareness of our own lives from her experience. Quechua mythology tells that there are spirits in many parts of nature, animals, birds, snakes, frogs, trees, stones, and more, but it does not say **you** are a spirit! A holy spirit! A divine spirit! You're not a body as many of you are taught to think. Miski's separation from her body tells us that. You are all spirits in Quechuan bodies learning your true nature through a material existence, not identities such as sons or daughters, brothers or sisters, husbands, or wives, nor identification with the body. You are each a spirit, an aspect of the One Great Spirit getting to know itself.

"Whoever knows themselves as a spirit beyond the body will never perish. The body may, but you won't.

"Just as Miski realized in dropping her body, so can we. Life is everlasting, beyond this material existence. We're spirits that live eternally. But most never return from the dead to explain this critical realization to others still alive. To do so is like the One Great Spirit as a trickster telling on itself, telling us our true nature **before** we would find out by separating from the body when death occurs. To know this before death destroys the fear of death. Fortunately for all of us, the spirit trickster is the one who drops a body and comes back to take up the same body and tell the living their true nature. Miski, you're that trickster.

"The unbelievable has happened before your eyes. Miski's body was dead for three days, and she reentered the body, bringing it back to life. She never died and never will. Only the body did. This realization is a new truth in your life. For some, maybe this was too much all at once. Enough said for such a life-changing day."

The villagers began mingling and talking, gathering around Miski. Others, still confused and with questions, approached Ch'askawani. The 'Precious One' knew there would be, thinking to himself that *existence is an unending beginning* if they only knew.

One of the first villagers to approach and address Ch'askawani was the highly respected elder Anka. He looked typical Quechuan in his attire with a multi-colored wool poncho and dark brown pants. His body was muscular and strong, yet a head full of gray hair and a face full of aging lines reflected his senior status. Even as an older man, Ch'askawani saw Anka's brown eyes ablaze with energy. Anka spoke first.

"You, my boy, are indeed the gift I am sure the Ch'asuq Pacha intended for us when they delivered you many moons ago. Raising the dead is unbelievable, an extraordinary thing that ideas we claim as our ability to know cannot explain.

"Not only have you shown us your ability as a gifted healer who will become well known and admired on that basis alone, but you are also a teacher of the highest order, able to explain what happened in clear words, enabling us to grasp it. You have my most profound respect."

"Your words show your respectfulness as well, Anka. What is ordinary and extraordinary to each of us has to do with what is familiar and unfamiliar. Witnessing the unfamiliar makes it extraordinary. With my ability to see a spirit outside the body and communicate with it without the spoken word, can you see how coaxing it back to the body would be familiar to me? Familiarity removes the 'extra,' leaving it ordinary."

"I see," Anka acknowledged, nodding.

"Life as you define it is your experience," Ch'askawani added, "All that we understand is limited to the ideas we hold. To be open to life beyond the fixed ideas currently held is when we experience something unfamiliar, like today, when we don't have ideas explaining it to ourselves. So, one of the lessons of today is to be open to what life has to show you."

Anka chuckled, "You cannot help but teach when you talk. Such a remarkable boy. Thank you for sharing ideas that we have been without, and being in our midst.

"My thanks to you, Anka, for accepting me as I am," Ch'askawani replied.

A middle-aged woman, Hamka, standing just to the right of Anka, was tall as Quechua women go, with intense eyes and a clear complexion. She wore a red shawl over a black sweater and a black skirt. But, unlike so many Quechuans, her hair color was brunette. She asked, "What further about this miracle may not be evident to us?

"Direct experience is the real teacher about existence, Hamka. What happened to Miski is her experience. What you were willing to see and hear was your experience. You are taught you live until you die. In believing that, you either question the experience that contradicts that belief, or question the belief. The course you choose will depend on whether your experience is direct, firsthand, or whether someone tells you about the experience. Direct experience establishes your truth. Hearsay demonstrates your belief.

"Those who were not here and only told of what happened today will never be as aware of it as you. You know what you saw. Another may gain a strong belief, but trust or confidence in someone about something not witnessed is a different basis entirely. Do you see the difference?"

"I do. Thank you," Hamka answered. "I have one more question. Is there anything else that we can derive from this incredible experience? Of course, I see that Miski could be considered holy by the rest of us. But, as a witness, is there more beyond this remarkable realization that I will never die?" Hamka asked.

"This realization of living forever is not going to sink in immediately. It will take a while for you to fully integrate this experience into a new reality that will come from it. Life will not change overnight for most. Otherwise, it would be an emotional upheaval.

Miski is no different from you, Hamka, or me, Anka, or anyone else. The same thing could happen to you or anyone here. You are glorified when you accept **you** are 'life everlasting.' You are not born. You do not die. You are not the body. The body is like a house that you inhabit until the experience provided is over, then you leave it. All of you are holy spirits in residence. You come into the physical world as that already. You forget because this awareness is under a heavy blanket of ideas that identify you as something else. Today's unique and strange experiences take you beyond common notions focused on the physical world. A wide crack opens between your thoughts, displaying qualities of a greater, more expansive you, which are available any time and exist simultaneously with the limited view of you. Understand then, what if a change in ideas of who you think you are and what you think life is changes everything? A different view creates a different you!

"So, there is hope for all of us," Hamka replied.

"Hamka, change, and expansion is the destiny of all. Rest assured," Ch'askawani uttered confidently.

"Thank you. What a blessing you are to us, Precious One," Hamka admitted and bowed as a show of respect.

An unending beginning. The resurrection of Miski was a significant event in Sonqollaqta. Naturally, the experience impacted the locals. Then, news of the event began to spread. At first, it trickled out. Then, as it spread, the village's unfamiliar name was heard by many. As a result, seekers of healing and seekers of truth began to trickle into the settlement.

Within several new moons, strangers from all directions were finding their way to the village to meet both the healer and the healed. Miski and Ch'askawani were both rarities in the world of Quechuan natives and projected a spotlight of attention on Sonqollaqta.

Because the number of travelers passing through Sonqollaqta was growing, Arisi was inspired to talk to Ch'askawani about permanent accommodations.

During a break while out in a potato patch cultivating, Arisi said to the young Ch'askawani, "I've been thinking, we cannot have these visitors laying around in the fields or leaning up against other villagers' houses. There are no locks on the doors, and some have expressed concern that strangers could steal stored food and personal items. We don't want curiosity to become a problem for the village. So, I have already talked to some of the villagers about building a compound of small rooms where visitors can stay, and a hall where you can meet with them and teach both travelers and interested villagers."

Nodding his head in agreement, the young boy responded with praise, "What a perfect idea and your reasoning is sound. Good thinking."

Arisi smiled and continued, "I selected a piece of land at the edge of the potato field a short distance behind the house. Several men have volunteered their labor and materials for the construction.

Ch'askawani smiled broadly, delighted with Arisi's attention to future considerations. "I am thankful you are planning and organizing efforts to build this compound that is needed, and happy that some of the villagers are willing to assist. Your ideas are in harmony with what the future holds. Thank you, Arisi. I appreciate your efforts."

The young boy was pleased, which made his poppy smile, and he replied, "Your future seems laid out. Kuychi and I have the unexpected privilege of attending to the details on the materialistic side, leaving you unburdened with participating in such matters and free to heal and teach, enabling you to live out your destiny!"

"And what is that?" Ch'askawani questioned.

"To become famous in this, your first life here!" Arisi enthusiastically responded.

"I see," Ch'askawani curtly replied.

Surprised by the boy's response, Arisi asked, "Does that not seem the outcome of what you can do for others?"

In his even tone, Ch'askawani commented, "Beloved Arisi, you presume my life, yours and Kuychi's are already created. In a sense, that's true, even in a deterministic way. But people have a way of unknowingly twisting the path to a destination, which accounts for the surprises. It's called free will. Remember, you achieve fame by good fortune or tragedy!"

The construction of the new compound proceeded exceedingly slow at first, much slower than desired or needed. Gathering stones for the walls was the most time-consuming undertaking and disheartening to the workers. Therefore, the men needed a solution to speed up the block-making process.

Arisi began experimenting with a novel idea of mixing mud with feathergrass. Shaping the mixture into a block required paddling with flat stones. The blocks were much lighter, and their uniformity made for more evenness in stacking blocks; the interlacing of blocks on the corners made for the sturdiness of the structure.

Workers would create a mud bath by mixing the simple ingredients of clay, water, and feathergrass. The process began by digging out a sizable area and filling it with clay and ample water to make mud. Then, to the earth, the workers added feathergrass to enable the clay to maintain a fixed shape once padded. The drying process took about a week in the dry season.

With four men making blocks daily, a steady supply of building blocks was continually available when needed. The roofs of all the structures were a lattice of branches overlaid with bundles of feathergrass stacked two deep.

The main hall and four small dormitories were completed by the rainy season, with the remaining dormitories finished by the end of the next dry season.

3

The events shared by the villagers are the richest in detail and the most memorable. Commonality is what Quechuan folklore captures, explaining how Miski made her way into the villager's folkloric tradition.

The inevitable end came for Miski when Ch'askawani was fifteen. She dropped her body the final time at one hundred ten years of age, having lived ten more fruitful years after her resurrection.

In those additional years, she received more attention, admiration, and care than in prior years. She had become dear to the hearts of so many villagers and outsiders who came to know of her. She became a symbol of a new view of life as unending, which took the curse of death and transformed it into a doorway opening to another life to experience, enabling others to realize that the supposed ending was a new beginning.

just another

One more time, the village residents and outsiders gathered around the deceased's body in front of Miski's house, appearing as a reenactment of ten years earlier. The one significant twist this time was the townspeople's mood, which was opposite of what it had been at her first funeral. This funeral was a celebration, the first of its kind, of the entire village honoring one of its own.

Miski's body was laid out as before, with Ch'askawani on one side of the body, staring straight ahead. The spirit of Miski was opposite the body, staring back at the boy, now a teenager. However, this time, Ch'askawani was translating the spirit's departing thoughts into audible words for all to hear.

A hush fell over the gathering as Ch'askawani began to speak, "Thank you for attending this extraordinary event. Although it is a burial service, it is more, a celebration. Totally unlike a similar occasion ten years earlier, the spirit you called Miski is here with us, out of her body. She has a parting message to share with all present. She will say to me what she wishes to say to you. In spirit, there is direct thought transmission from her to me. The thoughts she wishes to say will meld with my own. I will speak naturally, the steady flow of words appearing as if I'm speaking my thoughts, but they will be hers. So let us begin."

Ch'askawani took a deep breath, nodded, a signal to Miski's spirit to commence, and he began speaking.

"I LEAVE THIS BODY AND THIS LIFE FOR THE FINAL TIME WITH GREAT JOY RATHER THAN SORROW. I WILL ALWAYS BE WITH YOU, NOT VISIBLE TO THE NAKED EYE. THE UNSEEN IS WHO I AM AND WHO YOU ARE. WHEN PUTTING ON THE PHYSICAL FORM, WE APPEAR SEPARATE FROM EACH OTHER. BUT THAT'S BECAUSE WE FOCUS ON WHAT THE EYES SEE, SEPARATE PHYSICAL FORMS.

"KNOW IN YOUR HEARTS AND MINDS —YOU ARE ME DIFFERENTLY. WE ARE ALL THE SAME GREAT SPIRIT EXPERIENCING ITSELF IN THE INFINITE POSSIBILITIES IT CAN.

"IT IS FOR EACH OF US TO REACQUAINT OURSELVES WITH BEING THIS GREAT SPIRIT. NO ONE IS A BODY BUT A SPIRIT ACTING OUT DIFFERENT EXPRESSIONS IN DIFFERENT BODIES. UNDERSTANDING YOUR DIVINE NATURE IS TO BEGIN TO RESPOND MORE HARMONIOUSLY WITH THIS AWARENESS. THAT MEANS SEEING TO

THE WELLBEING OF ALL THROUGH THOUGHT, WORD, AND DEED.

"I AM SPEAKING THROUGH CH'ASKAWANI AS A MEDIUM, ONE OF THE CH'USAQ PACHA WITH US. MAY WE APPRECIATE HIS PRESENCE BY BEING MORE LIKE HIM.

"WHEN THE FOCUS IS ON THE PHYSICAL, YOU THINK PHYSICAL STRENGTH IS THE MOST POWERFUL FORCE, WHICH SHOWS THINKING IS THE REAL POWER BEHIND THAT THOUGHT. HOWEVER, SPIRIT KNOWS LOVE TO BE THE MOST POWERFUL FORCE, AS IT ACCEPTS ALL AS IT IS, WHICH ALMOST MAGICALLY CHANGES WHAT IS. WHEN LOVE BECOMES THE BASIS OF YOUR THOUGHTS, WORDS, AND DEEDS, YOU CREATE ANOTHER WORLD CALLED PARADISE. SUCH A WORLD MAY HAVE THE SAME APPEARANCE AS THIS WORLD, BUT WITH A CONTINUOUS JOY THAT IS CURRENTLY MISSING. YOU HAVE TO MAKE YOURSELF REFLECT THE DIVINE YOU ARE BY MAKING THIS WORLD A PARADISE. HEED MY WORDS. CHANGE YOURSELF FIRST, AND ALL ELSE AROUND YOU WILL EFFORTLESSLY CHANGE.

"I LOVE YOU ALL. I ALWAYS WILL. MAY YOUR HEARTS NOT BE TROUBLED. MAY THIS DAY BE A NEW BEGINNING. REMEMBER OF WHO YOU ARE AND ACT IN HARMONY WITH THAT.

"I END NOW, SAYING THANK YOU FOR SHARING THIS PRECIOUS LIFE WITH ME. MY RESURRECTION CELEBRATES A NEW AWARENESS OF LIFE; THAT WE ARE SPIRITS WHO LIVE FOREVER."

Ch'askawani raised his head and hands skyward. Closing his eyes, he said softly, "So it is."

Miski's lifeless body was carefully lifted along with the camelid skin beneath it and carried a short distance by several men to the gravesite originally dug ten years earlier alongside Miski's house.

The body interred; pallbearers rearranged the orchids on top of the overburden covering the body. Ch'askawani stood over the grave in silence after the pallbearers departed and finally conveyed telepathically to the spirit next to him, *feel free to go now. You are deeply loved and appreciated. You have done more for the evolution of consciousness in this village than you know. Thank you, Beloved, thank you.*

Ch'askawani walked away from the gravesite, smiling. He could hear people already celebrating.

The festival's purpose was to glorify the inhabitants of Sonqollaqta. Yet, there were almost as many 'visitors' as villagers present. Miski's resurrection facilitated by Ch'askawani was big news wherever it traveled and had put Sonqollaqta as a dot on the map of people's awareness.

Many women in the village created a song-n-dance to pay homage to Beloved Miski. The women in the background who did not perform, contributed the costumes worn by the dancers and singers. More than forty women, all wearing white billowy blouses, ornately colorful embroidered vests, black shirts with decorated hems, and a type of pillbox hat, also colorfully embroidered, danced in two long lines. A few women sang the most hauntingly beautiful melodies while the dancers twirled to the singing; the accompanying music was provided by musicians from Paucartambo.

Dancing, singing, laughing, drinking, and eating continued uninterrupted for three days, filling the high-altitude homeland with an atmosphere of gaiety, in stark contrast to the routine of daily life in the silent, rugged, and unforgiving terrain of the eastern slope of the Andean Mountains.

The festival became a regular affair put on every year, serving the dual purpose of commemorating Miski being raised from the dead, and announcing the end of the dreary and damp cold, wet season when Nature arose again from its dormancy, like Miski had from the dead.

Miski's anticipated death was also the year of the most unexpected beginning. Both Kuychi and Arise were in their early thirties, married more than fifteen years, and were childless. Everyone thought they had fertility problems, and so did they. But such was not the case.

Much to Kuychi's and Arisi's surprise she was found to be pregnant, and shortly after the end of the rainy season of the following year, she gave birth to a girl whom the parents named Ru'qu. Baby Ru'qu was long as most Quechuan babies go, with brown skin, straight black hair, and, to everyone's amazement, including parents, sparkling blue eyes. Moreover, she was healthy and very active as newborns go.

Ch'askawani adored Ru'qu. He was the only one who knew the spirit of Miski had reentered the physical world in the body of the baby Ru'qu.

In the Quechuan tradition, the person who fulfilled the role of priest and doctor, performing healing with the help of unseen forces, the supernatural, was called a shaman. Ch'askawani was a break with that tradition. Rather than referring to him as a shaman, the locals bestowed upon Ch'askawani the humorous title of *Apuiskayquechuankurku* (Great Spirit In A Quechuan Body) based on a statement he made the day of Miski's resurrection, when he indicated that everyone is the Great Spirit. He was the source of this playful title the villagers used to describe him. He encouraged it, knowing it a dubious title of respect; however true, it ironically kept him humble. He was aware everyone was the same Great Spirit, with varying degrees of awareness of that reality; meaning that everyone is to be treated with respect and value regardless of what level of understanding they possess. Everyone is a valuable part of the whole, as is every aspect of Creation. Everyone is in a state of becoming at their own pace.

Not only did Ch'askawani demystify his actions, making things transparent, but he also reinterpreted the traditional shaman's role. He was a counselor, an arbitrator and a therapist, supporting the well-being of all the villagers.

Undeniably, actions speak louder than words. Not only did healing give Ch'askawani more recognition, and his teachings endeared him, but Ch'askawani's compassion captivated others. When people bestowed food and material gifts upon him, he accepted them gracefully, only to turn around and give them to the needy that made their way to his door. He also used the food to feed strangers coming to the village seeking healing or wisdom.

Ch'askawani was a thief who had stolen the hearts of so many with his divine example. As a result, he achieved the highest recognition possible from the community. There was no pomp and pageantry of royalty; instead, immeasurable respect, reverence, devotion, and an air of equality were the atmosphere around him. In contrast to some of the villagers who sought control and power, Ch'askawani sought neither.

Another ten years passed. Respect, devotion, admiration, appreciation, and reputation grew as the boy became a young adult.

One day, Ch'askawani, now in his mid-twenties, was returning from his meditation in the mountains and was passing the field where Apo, in his late teens, was digging potatoes. It was harvest time. Apo was the son of Hamka and shared the feature of brunette hair with his mother. His face was round, and he had a thicker build than Ch'askawani.

Ch'askawani whistled at Apo, who looked up, saw his friend, and waved for him to approach. Ch'askawani diverted his route and walked along the edge of the field where the two met.

He observed Apo's difficult gait as he walked across the potato field, stiff and with a slight limp, making Ch'askawani wonder if something had happened. The pained expression on Apo's face confirmed his suspicion. "Apo, you're limping. What's wrong?"

Apo didn't say a word. Instead, without hesitating, he turned around and dropped his pants. Black and blue marks covered the backs of both his legs. Just as quickly, he pulled his pants up, turned back around, and said, "I am so angry at my tayta (father). He gets drunk regularly now with the Gang of Four in the thicket. Drunk out of his mind, he returns home and takes his frustration out on me! He won't touch mama. She's already warned him she'd leave him, and if provoked, mama would do it instantly."

"I am so sorry you have to experience such abuse," Ch'askawani said, consoling Apo. "What has produced the frustration? I heard from Arisi that Apichu's brother died some time ago; is that the issue?"

"You're right," Apo confirmed and further explained, "Tayta's twin brother died last year while in Paucartambo. Rumors circulating indicated murder. Whatever the cause of his brother's death, my poppy is deeply saddened, overcome with grief, and lately, he is just angry and drinking. It's as if it gives him the right to abuse me and others as a means of getting rid of his anger and frustration. I've had it. I cannot take anymore of him beating me. No. No more!"

Ch'askawani could see Apo was venting his built-up anger and, like his tayta, needed to get it out.

"Why does it have to be this way?" Apo shouted.

"In this world you cannot fully understand love unless touched by hatred. You cannot fully appreciate joy without being touched by sadness. Do you feel joy or sorrow when beaten?"

"I am suffering," Apo burst out. "Doesn't my tayta know beating me with a leather strap is painful for me?"

"There are two reactions to emotional and physical pain. One is compassion, not doing something you don't want to happen to you. For example, the pain of being beaten with a strap, you wouldn't do it to another."

"Right. So why does poppy do it then?" Apo begged, "He must know the pain he is inflicting."

"The other reaction," the Precious One indicated, "is reflected in the saying, hurt people hurt people. In other words, people..."

"I get it," Apo interrupted. "Tayta has felt pain before and seeks to inflict it on me. What satisfaction or pleasure is there in that?"

"Apichu does not know who is responsible for his twin brother's death and feels helpless in the matter. He wants to retaliate against someone, but who? He wants revenge, but against who? How does he get satisfaction for what he's lost?"

"I don't know!" Apo replied in frustration.

"He doesn't either."

"But why me?"

"He chooses someone who is least likely to return his destructive action in like-kind."

"Now I get it," Apo responded, "but why does it continue? Why can't he stop? I can't take this anymore!" Tears began to form in the boy's eyes. "It has even gotten worse with his drinking. Lately, he joins the Gang of Four two or three nights a week in the thicket. He gets drunk out of his mind. Then, when he comes home, he acts like a stranger, a different person!

"Apo, a hurting person cannot bury their pain and deny it, because it is energy; it resurfaces as cruelty, criticism, arrogance, disrespect, abuse, or inappropriate use of another. Apichu drinking messes with his mind and gives mental diversion and temporary relief from his pain. He beats you because it gives him temporary satisfaction in expressing his anger that drinking cannot provide. He's frustrated because there is no permanent relief from the anger he feels. The anger is really at himself. He feels inside something about himself, although his blame may focus outwardly. He is disappointed in himself. He feels powerless in not stopping his brother's death, which was an emotional loss, and powerless to find the one to focus his revenge on, which would enable him to feel powerful again."

"Thank you, Ch'askawani. I understand now. So, what can I do?"

"You move from weakness to strength when thinking and acting for the wellbeing of all involved."

"So, how do I do that?"

"When you start to take responsibility for your life, you are show-ing yourself and others what they need to do in their own lives. Currently, you are hurting because your tayta is hurting. Abuse will continue until someone breaks with the cycle of violence. You are the one who does it first for yourself. You start by realizing what you think is how you direct your life, and most of that is what you learned from being a young child. Both of us grew up in the Quechuan tradi-tion, a very successful adaptation to a harsh environment that has remained unchanged for thousands of years. That does not have to change as it deals with physical survival. However, the attitude toward life must change so the quality of life can change.

"The first attitude to consider is your attitude toward yourself. Who you think is more powerful than you is a possibility when you think that."

"You mean thinking my tayta is more powerful than me is just a thought that I keep thinking?"

"Yes; you are in control of your life. No one else is unless you think someone else is."

Apo objected, "He could beat me into submission or throw me out of the house. Then what would I do?"

"He's beating you now," the Precious One countered. "That's not working for him or you, and if you leave, your problem is not solved. So, you must allow Apichu to express himself, which will release the pain burdening him. But you cannot wait until he's drunk. I suggest you talk to him about the situation when he's sober. Tell him you are sorry about what happened to his brother, but beating you and destroying himself by drinking will not bring back his brother; that his own behavior is not only killing him, but the relationship he has with you and your mother, Hamka. Allow him to express his emotions when they arise. Then, even if he threatens to abuse you or attempts to, you can leave home permanently.

"Tell him you will not accept him beating you anymore. If it means you're out of the house, so be it. Doing all the work will be his consequence."

Then with deep concern, Apo asked, "But, what will happen to me?"

"Don't you have relatives who would love to have another pair of hands in the fields? Wouldn't you be compensated with food, just as is done now when you ask relatives to help?"

"Where will I live?"

"You can live in one of the small rooms in the compound," Ch'askawani affirmed. "I'll make room for you. You are more valuable to yourself and others than you know, Beloved Apo."

"But what if he threatens to beat you? You are just a young man, like me."

"That is my concern. Your life's lesson is to learn how to take care of yourself in all situations, starting with this one.

"When you are taking care of yourself, you are creating an environment around you where others will learn to take care of themselves. Hamka will learn from your actions. Your tayta will learn from your efforts.

"Destructive behavior is still a path to perfection, just a longer one. You help shorten that path for your poppy or anyone else who's destructive by being a creative example of a constructive path. No one is too young to learn. Replace fear with the inspiration of taking responsibility for yourself and encouraging others to take responsibility for themselves. Recognize it as a road to healing."

"Thank you, Ch'askawani. I have gained so much confidence and inner strength hearing your words," Apo expressed in appreciation for the guidance received.

"And you will gain even more in applying these words, Beloved Apo," Ch'askawani emphasized in a firm but loving matter.

"I will. Today, when I go back to the house," Apo added.

The boys embraced in loving friendship and parted, Apo back to digging potatoes with a newfound attitude toward his life; Ch'askawani headed to the compound to see what awaited.

After several steps, Ch'askawani stopped and turned in Apo's direction and yelled, "Apo, let me know how things work out. I think you'll be surprised."

Apo gave a thumbs-up in response. As he turned and walked to where he was digging, his mind was a great distance from harvesting potatoes. He felt the joy of a new perspective on his life, and the enthusiasm and confidence it instilled in him. Ch'askawani *was so right,* Apo thought; *a different attitude is a key to a new life. I was helping myself and helping others by example. The power of love is what* Ch'askawani *shows*—loving *myself and loving others. I see patience as caring for others even when they don't care about themselves. And I love myself even when things don't go as I would like. I give thanks to Ch'askawani. I thank myself for being willing to hear his meaningful words.*

Apo looked up into the endless blue sky for a while, requesting forgiveness for his past unmerciful actions from the Ch'usaq Pacha in silence.

Ch'askawani proceeded downslope toward the village on the meandering path separating fields of crops. He saw many villagers harvesting in their fields, thinking *that harvest is labor intensive. Entire families are in their crop patches uprooting potatoes and other edible tubers.* He saw many digging while others were shuttling tubers to their homes on their backs in shawls converted into sacks. The families with llamas would use them to carry the 'bags' of potatoes from field to house.

Ch'askawani knew Kuychi and Arisi were busy in their fields. *Even little Ru'qu would be there helping in any way she could,* he thought, *so, I'll give them a hand.* But then, something different came to him through his intuition, redirecting him. *Someone is waiting at the compound.* Feeling an urgency, he quickened his pace, thinking, I'll *stop to see Kuychi, Arisi, and Ru'qu'* in the *evening.*

As he passed behind Kuychi and Arisi's house, Ch'askawani observed two people sitting in front of the compound, a woman, and a man, both wrapped in blankets. Next, he noticed they were older, their gray hair showing. The couple saw Ch'askawani approaching and got up slowly. The woman was wearing a black shirt, a yellow sweater and a black umbrella with a yellow fringe. The man, who also looked well past middle age, was wearing dark knee-length pants and a colorful poncho over a red sweater. His movements were odd, Ch'askawani noticed. He was staring straight ahead and relying on the woman for assistance.

"Hello," Ch'askawani greeted them, "I'm Ch'askawani."

The woman spoke, "We've heard so much about you, young man. We've traveled some distance for your help. My name is Tuta, and my husband's, Catequil." She was robust, as many Quechuan women are because of the physical work. However, she had a plain face with wrinkled skin, and her hair was a mixture of black and gray.

"Nice to meet you, young man," Catequil said as he extended his hand for a handshake. They shook hands. Ch'askawani noticed he had large muscular hands and a strong build, a long nose and big eyes, and streaks of black in predominantly gray hair. *A pleasant face* thought Ch'askawani and said, "The pleasure is mine, Catequil. Please, Beloveds, come inside. Let me carry your blankets."

Ch'askawani gathered their two blankets in his arms and proceeded ahead of them to open the door, allowing them to pass inside.

"Please sit on the log near the hearth. I'll add some wood so you may warm yourselves. There is a bed over in the corner for you to rest later and, please, Beloveds, feel free to stay the night or even two if you like. I'll provide food for you." Then Ch'askawani stepped over to a small pile of wood near the door and brought several pieces to stoke the fire. He stepped to one side so as not to come between his guests and the heat the renewed fire was putting out.

"Our home is in the Urubamba River valley," Tuta began to explain. "It has taken us several days on foot to finally get here. We didn't prepare for the cold nights in the mountains. Fortunately, the wool blankets we carried were additional protection. It was slow going with my husband. He is blind and has been for a few years. Blindness is a great debility for him and a great hardship for me. We have only two children. They and I do all the work. They are grown and have enough of their own chores to do. They are at our place now, harvesting crops. They are very generous with their help. Hearing about you only recently, they thought best we come right away. They would look after things until we returned." Tuta sighed deeply, saying, "You are our last hope for returning my husband's eyesight. Please, Ch'askawani, we heard you can raise the dead. Surely you can restore my Catequil's sight. "

"I am so sorry to hear of your hardships, Dear Ones," the young healer replied, adding, "It all has to do with your willpower."

When Tuta mentioned her husband's blindness, Ch'askawani began psychically scanning Catequil's head and saw no organic reason for his blindness. Instead, it was some trauma he had experienced. He knew the key to healing was Catequil's will. Stepping in front of him, Ch'askawani asked, "Catequil, can your blindness be corrected? And do you believe I can heal you?

"Yes, to both questions, young man," Catequil replied, "We would never have undertaken this strenuous journey on foot, which has been difficult and tiring, if I didn't believe I can regain my sight with your help, which is saving my life!"

"It is by your fate, by your will power alone that makes it so. Please close your eyes," Ch'askawani requested. Then He put his hands over Catequil's eyes. The two men stood in silence for a considerable time. Catequil felt his head getting hot. Finally, Ch'askawani removed his hands from the older man's eyes and commanded Catequil, "Open your eyes and SEE."

The older man blinked his eyes a couple of times, then yelled, "I CAN SEE! TUTA, I CAN SEE!" as he bolted for the doorway and looked out. I CAN SEE, he yelled. Then, he turned around, jumping up and down, and inadvertently ran to Tuta, who was crying uncontrollably. He threw his arms around her, hugged her tightly and yelled, "I GOT MY SIGHT BACK, TUTA! I am so happy!" Then turned to Ch'askawani and gave him a big hug. "You saved my sight and my life. How can I ever thank you? You're a miracle worker! Such a healing is amazing!"

Then Tuta, who was still in tears, hugged Ch'askawani, who smiled broadly and remained quiet until the hyper-discharge of energy dissipated.

Then, he spoke to both Tuta and Catequil, who had calmed down enough to listen, "Those who have seen what before was unbelievable become messengers of a new vision of the possibilities life holds. Both of you are now people who carry that news."

Both listeners nodded in agreement.

Still excited, Catequil asked, "How did you do it?"

Ch'askawani's response was, "I was about to ask you the same question."

"What do you mean?" Tuta asked.

"Simply this," Ch'askawani said; "if your husband had said 'no, I don't believe I will be able to see again,' there would have been nothing I could have done! You wouldn't even have come here! I only could assist him in what **he wanted to happen**. He's the one who had the faith that he could see again. HE DIDN'T THINK HE WAS CAPABLE OF DOING IT HIMSELF; HE THOUGHT HE COULD WITH MY HELP, so you two created the possibility to make that happen by coming here to see me. Does that make sense?

"Yes, I just never thought that way before," Tuta replied.

"So, you are saying we eliminate possibilities by the ideas we choose to think?" Catequil inquired.

"Beloved, you just answered your question," Ch'askawani answered, smiling.

Tuta just looked on.

"But it still is so amazing. I still want to imagine you did it and will say so!" Catequil exclaimed.

Ch'askawani just laughed, there was nothing more to say.

True to his statement, Catequil ran outside and shouted to the heavens, "I CAN SEE. I CAN SEE. I CAN SEE. CH'ASKAWANI DID IT. HE DID IT! YEEHAW!"

Tuta and Ch'askawani followed Catequil outside, stood, and watched with joy at Catequil's wild gyrations as if in a dance. Catequil could not contain his excitement. Happiness consumed him.

Of course, a commotion would draw attention, and it did. So, in a potato patch a short distance away, Arisi, Kuychi, and Ru'qu heard the shouting. They stopped working and hurried down to the patch's lower edge, where the compound was located. There, they saw Catequil still dancing around as they approached. When Catequil saw them, he yelled, "HE DID IT. CH'ASKAWANI DID IT. I WAS BLIND, NOW I CAN SEE! HE'S AMAZING!

Hearing the outcome was no surprise to Ch'askawani's family.

Catequil carried on for a bit longer, then suddenly stopped, as he was exhausted by his reverie.

By that time, several more villagers were on the scene asking questions, and once they found out, there were more congratulations. By that time, Catequil was spent, standing quietly next to Tuta, with a massive smile from ear to ear.

Everyone became quiet as Ch'askawani spoke, "What a wonderful occasion as Beloved Catequil, who was blind, can see again. An unexpected lesson for all can be taken from his experience; that life disappoints you to broaden your view. It sounds odd, doesn't it? Yet consider the answers to these questions: Was Catequil aware his eyesight could be saved had he never gone blind? Would he have gained a fuller appreciation of the gift of sight had he not lost his sight? Would he have the zest for life we've just seen him display had he not gone blind and regained his sight? Instead, his disappointment at being blind, in the end, was converted into ecstasy. This lesson is another gift life has bestowed upon Beloved Catequil today. And for those of us witnessing this marvel, remember, when things don't go your way, allow disappointment to open you to see that unimagined possibilities are already on the way. Life is taking you a way that you never imagined possible."

Arisi and Kuychi just shook their heads, amazed by the profound insights Ch'askawani could convey. Arisi thought, *this young man is so incredible. Quechuan folklore will never recount all that he has said and done. Never.*

The news of a visitor who came to the village blind and walked away with his sight, thanks to Ch'askawani, spread through Sonqollaqta like fire. The young healer had performed many healings, but returning someone's sight was his first of its kind.

4

In his thirty-fifth year, Ch'askawani was pleased, witnessing significant and sustained changes in the attitudes and actions of many villagers over the previous thirty years. They had opened their hearts, revealing greater compassion, extraordinary kindness, tremendous respect, and greater love. The prime mover of their new direction was none other than Ch'askawani.

The quarterly village gatherings where Ch'askawani spoke, were a resounding success. One memorable meeting took place that year, on a beautiful dry season afternoon, at the usual circular area in the southern portion of the village designated for community functions. However, as the community grew, the meeting area had been enlarged.

Those in attendance brought their camelid skins to sit on, gathering in a large circle with Ch'askawani standing in the middle when he spoke. The younger kids sat on adult laps while the teenagers usually sat together on the periphery. The crowd was very colorful. The women wore sweaters of red, orange, yellow, and light blue and all in umbrella hats that were black with the same yellow fringe, with men in tans, blues, browns, purples, and blacks, and the traditional wool hats with earflaps, some with tassels hanging from the flaps.

"Thank you for coming to this meeting," Ch'askawani began, "The village has grown in the number of inhabitants, but more importantly, a noticeable personal growth in your views about life, affecting your relationships and how you react! I hope these meetings contribute to each feeling better about yourself and the people in your lives. And, clearly, the focus has shifted from what happens to you to how you respond to what happens. So today, the talk is about your identity, which is how you define yourself.

To Ch'askawani, the audience looked relaxed and attentive, showing an eagerness to hear what he would say.

"You are beyond the definitions given to you since birth. You are the unchanging spirit who watches changes taking place throughout your life. If you define yourself by changing things, you will experience self-worth as ups and downs. Sometimes you like yourself, and sometimes you hate yourself.

"The idea that you like yourself or another likes you when you do something that makes you feel good or makes someone else feel good, or you dislike yourself or others dislike you when you do something that you regret, or others disapprove of, all of it reflects the ups and downs you all have experienced. A world of judgment comes into existence where everyone learns to judge themselves and everyone else. The ideas you are taught and obey are how you control yourself.

"You appear to handle yourself. But the source of ideas is tradition. Tradition is the basis of your self-talk, keeping you in harmony with others. When tradition is gone against, you hate yourselves, which is more common than loving yourselves when you do wrong. But understand that the thoughts, feelings, and desires that create these ups and downs are not you. You are not these changes in thoughts, feelings, and desires. You are just witnessing them. They do not affect you unless you identify them **as you**. So, I am telling you that you are not who you think you are.

"Miski told those gathered who watched her return from the dead, about her experience without a body; that she didn't need to breathe, nor eat, nor sleep nor even move. She only needed to think to make anything happen instantly, and when there was no thought, she had no experience, but she still existed. Even now, though her body is underground, her spirit still lives.

"To put it in simple terms, are you the poncho or the shawl you carry around?"

Ch'askawani saw many of the villagers' heads nodding as he looked around the circle and repeated words he had said years earlier.

"And neither are you these thoughts, feelings, and desires you carry around in your heads. You are a formless witness of life, a spirit witnessing change. You have taken on a body, like putting on a pair of pants or a skirt, to watch experience, not identify as it.

"For example, Am I hungry? Are you or is the body hungry? Am I hurt? Are you? Or is your body hurt? I feel bad. Do you? Or is it a thought you have learned?

"Free yourself from identification as the body. Free yourself from the identification as thoughts. Free yourself from identification as feelings. Free yourself from identification as desires. When you have freed yourself from these things, what will you be free to do?"

Ch'askawani paused. He wanted to let the question sink in, and the energy of curiosity build.

Then, after a few moments, in a loud voice, he answered his rhetorical question: "**You are free to love!**"

He paused again for the impact he wanted. He knew what stopped people from loving each other were thoughts, feelings, desires!

Then he repeated his previous statement, **"You are free to love…
which is being your true self**. It does not identify as thoughts, feelings, and desires that **are not you! Love is the activity of Divinity
being itself."**

"Love is your true nature. Yet that love has been hidden under a
heavy blanket of thoughts, feelings, and desires over many, many
years. When everyone is loved and expresses love, only love is
seen. No one can control love. It is only amplified with giving and
receiving. A world of love is in the making, a world where thoughts,
feelings, or desires no longer separate us —we're united by love."

Although Ch'askawani's words struck a positive chord with many, a
few, not wanting to be identified, were silently disgruntled. Kichka,
Manqu, Waywa, and Yanamayu, all in their mid-to-late-forties, were
among them. Even though hungover to one degree or another, having drunk excessively for over twenty-five years, and now alcohol-
ics, they still attended the meetings. They viewed the change in
the village as a direct threat to their existence. The four men were
at the villagers' gatherings because of paranoia, afraid they would
be talked about, and actions would be taken against them by the
collective to stop their antics. The fact remained, they were only
projecting their self-judgments on others and fantasizing about an
outcome.

They had taken on a habit that was destroying them ever faster,
eroding their desire to change and covering what they presumed to
be their secret. But the homosexual activities of the Gang of Four
were witnessed by many over the years.

If these men were trying to hide their actions, they were doing a
poor job of it. They were out of their minds when drunk and were
seen on many different occasions by different villagers kissing one
another and having sex together while in altered states of consciousness. They were no real threat to anyone but themselves.

However, two other detractors, Guari and Atoc, didn't like Ch'askawani or his messages. They, too, wanted change but in an altogether different direction and to that end, Ch'askawani was a roadblock.

Other than wearing the traditional Quechua clothing of dark wool pants, colorful poncho, and cap with earflaps, no two men could appear more opposite to their neighbors. Guari was taller and fatter than most men, looking like he never missed a meal. He had a round face, bulging cheeks, deep-set eyes, a large nose, and a large mouth. Atoc was equally tall but with a slim physique, narrow head, long nose with bony cheeks, and beady eyes. Their brown skin and black hair completed a sinister appearance.

As an aside, Arisi found out much later from Manqa that they had cozied up to the Gang of Four with the intent of enlisting them in their efforts to undo somehow the changes Ch'askawani was advocating in Sonqollaqta. Manqa revealed background information not well known about the two 'foreigners,' "Guari and Atoc originally claimed they had heard of Ch'askawani and wanted to be part of a community that had a progressive vision."

While listening to Manqa tell that, Arisi recalled, *the men came ten years earlier. Both were arrogant and condescending in their* communication, *and so distrusted. Nevertheless, they staked their claims to land that no one else owned or used, and got help to construct their houses. And so, their lives began in Sonqollaqta as farmers, but there was much more to their settling here.*

"Honestly, by any stretch of the imagination, the two men are not farmers. They aren't interested in hard work as we know it. They came from Qosqo, a large urban area where the ruling class taxed people, requiring a portion of their crops as a tribute to expand their power and empire.

"That social order being to their liking, they want to be part of the ruling class somewhere! So, Guari and Atoc came here to install the same plan as the beneficiaries, of course, on a much smaller scale, to make their dream come true. Once installed, they would hook up with the much more extensive political network in Qosqo, which would expand that empire to the eastern slope! Our lives wouldn't be ours after that!

"According to Guari, a stumbling stone to their plan was Ch'askawani," Manqa explained, adding, "That's what he told Kichka, Waywa, Yanamayu, and me, anyway. Ch'askawani could not be deceived or manipulated by false flattery or dubious gifts, and they knew it, which made the young man a formidable opponent in their eyes. Moreover, Ch'askawani was not political, but his proposed vision had political implications that did not align with their plans."

Returning to Ch'askawani, after a few moments of silence, he continued, "You, spirit, are constantly expanding. You cause your existence. You are the Creator who creates to know itself. If you look at one of your hands, the Great Spirit represents the palm. The fingers and thumb are extensions of that one hand.

In the same way, you are an extension of the Great Spirit so that it can experience itself in a multitude of courses simultaneously. The Creator is each of us uniquely to enable us to share all these differences simultaneously. As the Great Spirit, you are ever-expanding spirits who drop bodies and pick up other bodies to experience growth and different situations. All these experiences enable the Great Spirit to become more aware of itself. Understand, each of us is the Great Spirit interacting with others who are themselves the same Great Spirit!

"The very nature of the Great Spirit is the love of itself as it includes all. It is continually expanding to love all that it is becoming. Consider this, an animal in its natural state is wild. All its activities, it does naturally. Animals like us have spirits. To tame wild animals, breaking their 'spirit' is necessary. The animal is trained not to continue to do what it has done in the wild. Training the animal is the means of destroying its instinct. The idea is to get the animal to accept new conditions, new rules which change its life.

"The same thing happens to the spirits who are in human bodies; you, a spirit, are 'broken' like a wild animal is tamed. As a child, you're coerced into certain habits, identities, and repeatedly occurring patterns and punished for things you are not to do, while rewarded for things expected of you. None of this is in harmony with your true nature. As a result, your energy, while expansive, is confined to particular habit patterns. In other words, you are taught not to do what comes naturally. You don't even know what that is.

"You are told you are the body, and given a name and other identities like boy or girl, man or woman, son or daughter, husband or wife, father or mother, parent or child, and there are specific responsibilities with each label. Then, as life goes on, the identities change, and you act differently with each identity. For example, you are one way when single; when married, another.

"The repetition of these patterns becomes a tradition. Please understand, I am not saying the accepted practice is wrong. However, while the Quechuan tradition has successfully adapted to harsh environments like the Sonqollaqta location, the repetitive patterns have led to a life of monotony and boredom that contribute to unhappiness, unkindness, and unloving dispositions. Coerced by the social pressure of tradition, you accept specific ideas, attitudes, actions, patterns, and timing as important. This repetition may cause anger, frustration, carelessness, resentment, discontent, an intense self-dislike for having these feelings, or hatred toward others for forcing you to accept things, all of which can lead to self-destructive, negative habits that appear to keep you going. But hurting people hurt themselves and hurt other people. Violence and abuse both occur, foreshadowed by self-abuse.

"Now I ask you, are the highlights of Quechuan tradition recounted in folklore? And don't these stories represent the values we wish to pass on to generations that follow?"

Ch'askawani paused, took off his hat, removed his poncho, and looked around for responses to his questions. Many heads were nodding, which was his indication to proceed.

"Then I ask you, in the sacred Quechuan oral tradition called folklore, was it said, you are to treat your spouse as a servant? Can you make and or carry out threats to hurt another person? That you are to make another person afraid by using looks, actions, gestures, smashing things, destroying another's possessions, abusing pets, and displaying weapons? Can you put another person down? Can you make a person feel bad about themselves? Can you humiliate a person by calling them names? Can you make a person feel guilty? Can anyone tell me, have these words ever been spoken in the oral tradition? Beloved Ones, it does not say these things. These are the actions of hurting people who hurt people."

He stopped and noticed the deathly silent gathering. Ch'askawani allowed silence to continue for many moments. He could hear whimpering, crying, sniffling, apologies offered, and responses of forgiveness. Victims and victimizers were present.

"Now, the hurting people know who they are, and so does everyone else. Making light of such abuse and not taking the painful cries of others as important must come to an end. Nor can you deny it is happening. Nor can you shift responsibility for your abusive actions on those abused. Hurting people hurt themselves and hurt other people."

Guari leaned over to Atoc and whispered, "We are going to have to do something about this guy if our plan is ever to work." Atoc looked at Guari and nodded in agreement.

"The time has come to glorify the Quechua Oral Tradition and glorify yourselves," Ch'askawani offered. "Any change in your life begins by forging a new view. To see life anew will ignite an explosion in you. When your idea of everything changes, everything changes for you. True happiness is living in your natural state of love. Do not be tied to thoughts, feelings, or desires. They only hinder your expansion. Be genuine and ordinary like the birds. Open your wings to the vastness of the sky. The ideas you identify as, forget. Just be satisfied with who you are, eternally the Great Spirit. When your desire is what you have, it becomes satisfaction. There is no more desire. You have you.

"The hardships, the pain, and the suffering will all end. You imagine limiting things because you have nothing but that to experience. You are the absolute perfection of the Great Spirit. You are here to see the experiences occurring, not identify them and make them into a story!"

Thinking he had presented a huge number of thoughts to mill over, Ch'askawani considered that as a good place to stop and said, "Enough for today. You have a lot to think about."

As the gathering started to break up, Ch'askawani's attention focused on Arisi, Kuychi, and Ru'qu sitting together chatting quietly, when he heard his name called from behind. He turned around to see Apo, walking in front of his parents, Hamka and Apichu, approaching. They were all smiling.

"Thank you, Ch'askawani. The words seem not enough," Apichu said. "You have made me see the grave error in my ways. I have begged my son and my wife for forgiveness. It has lifted a great burden from me."

Hamka jumped in immediately, "Yes, thank you, Precious One. You have helped my son and my husband, which has helped me, and we are a better family for it."

"You are amazing!" Apo added.

"Why is life so difficult at times?" Apichu asked.

"If a leaf goes in the direction of a stream's flow, is its movement not effortless?" Ch'askawani asked in response.

"Yes."

"But many people have the desire to go upstream against the natural flow. They want a challenge, or they feel dead. There is death, but it is only the end of desires, thoughts, and feelings. It is a desire for a challenge that makes the heart hard to open and makes it impossible for you to love, dance, sing, and be happy. If you proceed the effortless way, you are not being lazy. Thoughts forced on the mind will take you far away from who you are. You identify as the challenge, not the Great Spirit you are.

"Understand this, Apichu. You are perfect now, just as Hamka and Apo are. But these words are not found in your oral tradition, or your upbringing. Each one of you is ever-being and ever-becoming. That is the course of expanding love. You don't need to try to be what you already are. You are like a dog chasing its tail; nothing to gain by such effort. Just forget everything. Be who you are. No thoughts. No feelings. No desires. Just live. Just love.

"Take a lesson from the birds in nature. You will not find distinctions among the birds. Not one weak, another, strong. Not one happy, another sad. They just live without being hindered by such thoughts! So go in peace, my Beloved Ones."

Ending, Ch'askawani noticed many had been listening to the conversation and nodded they had understood.

"Blessings to all of you!" Ch'askawani shouted.

"And to you, Ch'askawani!" Were the thankful replies.

Looking at Arisi, Kuychi, and Ru'qu, their camelid skins in arms ready to depart, the Precious One walked up to them and embraced each of them. Unexpectedly, to Arisi and Kuychi's surprise, he stared into Ru'qu's blue eyes for what seemed like an endless moment. He realized that she had grown up almost unnoticed by him in that instant. At *the young age of twenty*, he thought *she is taller than most Quechua women and men. She has a strong, slender, muscular body hidden under those loosely fitting and layered garments she wears. Her straight, long, shiny, black hair, braided in the traditional style, and dark skin make her appear* like *any other Quechua Indian woman. But her blue eyes sparkle and* provide *a mesmerizing appearance. Those blue sapphire eyes in a population of brown-eyed people give her a fascinating aura of mystery. She radiates vigor, confidence, and strength of spirit. And, what an attractive face.*

"Ch'askawani?" Arisi asked for attention, interrupting the young man's musings.

He quickly turned to Arisi, "Yes?" Then just as quickly turned back to Ru'qu and said, "You have qualities that will make you an influence with the people in the village. You are developing wisdom and compassion, which means your words of guidance will be accepted and respected."

Ch'askawani's attention on Ru'qu made wonderful what he might have psychically seen in her past.

"Thank you for your kind words, Ch'askawani," was the short reply by Ru'qu. She was quiet and pensive by nature, qualities she shared with her mother.

Ch'askawani again quickly returned his gaze to Arisi and asked, "What did you want to say?"

"From what you said this afternoon, the impression I get is that there is nothing to do beyond letting go of most of what has been fed to us, which limits us," Arisi commented.

"What you say is true, but it's not as if what you have learned is wrong. Everything is perfect for each person at each moment. Be grateful, not for what something is, but how it inspires you. Value it for propelling your spiritual growth as perfect as life is. So, you could call it letting go, or you could see it as receiving what is always there to access instead of thoughts, feelings, desires, fears, and regrets. In other words, your intuition.

Here's what I am suggesting. Everything is of value for your spiritual growth. The mechanism of life looks like the action of a bow and arrow. The bow is the situation. Your participation in whatever is happening is like pulling back the arrow, which leads to hardship; it's not the direction of happiness. When you finally let go, the distance and speed the arrow travels toward the intended target, say happiness, is determined by how far back you pull, or the amount of hardship you experience. But that release in life is more subtle than a bow and arrow. Like releasing the hand, **letting go of everything** in life propels you forward spiritually, which is valid for all of you."

"I see, like carrying a heavy load of wood out of necessity. Then, when it is released, you feel lighter than when burdened with the load," Arisi interpreted.

"Yes, exactly!" Then Ch'askawani, in a quieter and softer tone of voice, said, "Can I tell you a secret?"

The listener's eyes opened wide in response.

He leaned toward them and whispered, "You may think you are living, but could it be you are 'being lived'?"

"What does that mean, Beloved Ch'askawani?" Kuychi asked. The same question was on the minds of Arisi and Ru'qu.

"Think of life as a snow-capped mountain and the only portion you see is the snow cap. The remainder is the invisible portion of life. That means what you see is only a tiny portion of what is happening and accessible.

As a spirit, you live in a body. Other invisible spirits are always around you without bodies assisting in making decisions, offering suggestions, and reminding you to do things. For example, when you think you get a brilliant idea, do you ever wonder where you got it? A spirit guide gave it to you.

Spirit guides do everything with you so seamlessly, you don't even know it is happening. You imagine it's **you**! So, you are never alone, although it may appear you are at times. You may feel alone when you have isolated yourself by ignoring the spirits always with you.

"You are guided effortlessly through life IF you are listening. That is what is meant by 'being lived.' Listening is the key. Developing the skill to listen to others and listen to yourself is no more than listening to your spirit guides speaking to you, often through you and through others to you! But people who don't feel good about themselves, don't trust their thoughts, decisions, or insights are making a grave error. They are missing out on the wisdom coming from a much more significant portion of existence."

"Wow, Ch'askawani! What an incredible insight!" Arisi exclaimed.

"The other villagers definitely would benefit from hearing this," Kuychi offered.

"Are we all endless streams of insight once we tap into this larger part of us?" Ru'qu' asked.

"Indeed, Miss Blue Eyes, indeed." Ru'qu smiled shyly.

Meanwhile, not many footsteps away, Guari was stirring the hot coals of paranoia among the already discontented Gang of Four. "Sounds like you guys have chosen the wrong path from what young Ch'askawani has said."

Manqu squinted his eye, wondering, *what are these two guys after?*

"You guys have been hearing this kid preach for much longer than we have. Aren't you tired of hearing him yet?" Atoc asked, looking over where Ch'askawani was standing, trying to get the goat of one of the Gang of Four.

"Maybe there is something to what the kid is saying?" Manqu offered.

"You must be kidding," Waywa contested. "That stuff is for people who live in the stars. If he thinks he will change this world, he's crazy! He certainly isn't going to change me. That's for sure!"

"Who'd want to change you? You're so sweet now," Kichka said mockingly.

"Oh, shut up, would you," Waywa fired back.

"Boys, boys, why are you arguing among yourselves? Maybe we can put our heads together and relieve the entire village of this problem once and for all," Guari suggested, trying to get the four men to focus on his interest.

"What are you suggesting?" Yanamayu asked.

Looking over in Ch'askawani's direction, Guari suggested, "Maybe it's time for this guy to disappear. I mean, isn't it the way to get things back to the way they used to be?"

"What do you mean?" Manqu asked.

"People minding their own business and not caring what other people are doing. If people get beaten or abused, it's because they deserve it. If you want to get drunk, that's your business. Who should care?" Guari reasoned.

"He's got a good point," Kichka responded mindlessly.

"Just think about it, boys," Guari said in his smooth persuasive tone as he motioned to Atoc it was time to depart.

Ch'askawani, looking between Arisi and Kuychi, noticed the discussion taking place, including the six men. He knew fate was rearing its head.

Arisi looked at Kuychi and Ru'qu and said, "I have some business to discuss with Ch'askawani. If you two want to go, I'll see you back at the house."

Kuychi looked at Ru'qu, who nodded. Then, she looked back at Arisi and said, "Yes, love. We'll head home now. Thank you, Ch'askawani, for a very inspiring afternoon."

Smiling, Ch'askawani replied, "You're welcome, Me-You!"

Kuychi smiled broadly and, with Ru'qu, walked away.

The Precious One asked, "What business, Beloved Arisi?"

Arisi, looking in the direction of the women leaving, said, "Seeing you staring at Ru'qu brought to mind a curiosity I've had over the years but never seemed to remember to ask you about until now."

"What about her?" Ch'askawani inquired, already aware of what was going to be said.

"Yes, from a very early age, Ru'qu's knowledge was dumbfounding. She picked up Quechua too quickly and showed an unexpected familiarity with everyone in the village at the first meeting and the locations of houses. It struck me as odd. I considered asking you more than once, but you were never present when the thought came to me. Were my guides making me aware of something? Not knowing about my spiritual guardians, I didn't have that thought before. Is there something more to it than just me? Or was it just that she was a bright little girl?

"I wondered when you would ask?" Ch'askawani noted. "You were right to wonder. The familiarity with things she possessed was a clue. But of what, you ask. The short answer is Ru'qu' is Miski's spirit come back into a body!"

Arisi responded with raised eyebrows, "Wow, that makes sense, but I would never have guessed that. I guess the evidence of life is continuous, and probably all around us if we were more aware."

Ch'askawani simply nodded.

A couple of days later, in the early evening, the sun had bid the mountains farewell as night obscured the landscape. The cold that characterized the nighttime was already making itself felt.

Ch'askawani was stoking the fire in the hall when he heard chaotic voices approaching his door. He turned toward the doorway and saw two silhouettes in the dark who sounded drunk and who appeared to be leaning against one another—then identified Manqa moaning in pain. The other person was Waywa, who had an arm around Manqa's waist, holding him up. Waywa was hardly coherent as he spoke, "Manqa was...he tried...a tree...he fell...shoulder."

Ch'askawani quickly went to the door to help Waywa bring Manqa inside.

"Let's sit him down on this log by the fire. He feels cold," the Precious One directed Waywa.

"My...my...rrrrrrrr right shoulder rrrr," Manqa said, flinching in pain.

"Ok, we'll need to remove your shirt so I can see the exact spot of the pain," Ch'askawani explained.

Manqa fumbled with his good arm to remove the wool pullover. Waywa was useless as he stood in a stupor. Ch'askawani maneuvered Manqa's good arm out of the sweater, then over his head, and finally pulled it gently off the arm of the painful shoulder. Immediately, Ch'askawani could see the break in the bone running from the shoulder to the neck. The bone had not broken through the skin. Then he looked up at Waywa, who, without a word, suddenly turned, almost falling as he staggered to the doorway and disappeared into the darkness. Ch'askawani thought, there's *no use stopping him. He's had years of experience getting around drunk in the dark.*

Manqa moaned in pain, "Please help me!"

"Just try to sit calmly and don't move more than you have to," instructed Ch'askawani, adding, "I do not put conditions on healing someone until this moment. You've been slowly destroying your body and your will to live for more than twenty-five years. That's your choice, of course. It's my choice whether to enable you or not. I will not support what you are doing to yourself."

"You... won't...heal me?" Manqa asked, disappointedly.

"Make no mistake, Beloved Manqa, I will heal you completely, but on one condition only."

"What?" Manqa, almost pleading, asked.

"You give up drinking alcohol. No more alcohol. No more. That means your drinking days are over, or you leave here the way you came in—drunk and in pain. Do you understand?" Ch'askawani's words were firm and uncompromising.

"Stop the pain. Please heal me. I'll do anything," Manqa begged.

"I want to hear you say, I will stop drinking alcohol from this moment. I will give you some time to think it over. It's an important decision. The biggest change you will make in this life. I will step outside and wait for your decision," Ch'askawani indicated. He turned and walked through the doorway. Standing out in the dark was chilling.

He could hear Manqa's moaning and groaning. Ch'askawani thought the pain would sober him, and *the more clear headed he is, the more pain he'll feel. As the pain worsens, the easier his decision will become.*

Before long, Manqa surrendered by yelling out, "Ok, Ch'askawani, ok! You win! I'll stop drinking alcohol. Please, heal me! I'll be forever in your debt."

Ch'askawani stepped back inside and walked over to Manqa, looking him straight in the eyes and confirming his pledge, "You said no more drinking alcohol, ever?"

"No more drinking alcohol, **ever**," Manqa reiterated, "Now, please, please take this pain from me!"

"As you request. Healing the bone will not take long. Yet, the healing will cause pain of its own, but it will subside, and the healing will be complete; the bone will be as if the shoulder were never broken," Ch'askawani assured Manqa.

"Is that possible?" Manqa asked.

"Yes, you will see for yourself," Ch'askawani answered confidently, "So, let us begin."

Ch'askawani walked over to the woodpile and selected a stick which he brought back to Manqa, and said, "I want you to close your eyes and focus your attention on the broken bone, visualize it whole. Then, when you start to feel almost unbearable pain put this stick between your teeth and bite down on it as hard as you can."

As Manqa closed his eyes, he took the stick and bit down on it. Ch'askawani moved around behind him, first putting his left hand with six fingers over the top of the break without touching it. Then the right hand over the top of the left hand. This extraordinary healer concentrated all his energy on the bone-break under his hands. Radiated from his hands, the energy became a ball of hot light, intensifying the heat in Manqa's right shoulder. Manqa moaned as he bit down harder on the stick than he thought possible. The heat was like putting his shoulder in boiling water.

"Just hold on, Manqa, hold on," Ch'askawani encouraged him, "A little bit longer. Hold on. Hold on. Hold on."

Manqa's jaw was so tight; it was unbearable. He thought he had bitten the stick in two. He was becoming delirious, feeling his whole body on fire.

"One more moment, Ch'askawani yelled, then, "There, it is done!"

Manqa was sober and sweating profusely.

"Just remain seated and rest. Your shoulder will cool," Ch'askawani advised, adding, "As the inflammation in the shoulder subsides, the pain will also. It may surprise you there will be no evidence that your fall broke the bone."

Manqa smiled, thinking to himself, *the intense heat felt like it burned the alcohol out of my body.*

"It did," Ch'askawani responded unexpectedly.

"You read my thoughts!" Manqa blurted out.

"Yes, I did. Didn't I tell you the healing would be complete?"

5

No day at high-altitude in the dry season south of the equator is ordinary. The sun's heat quickly displaces the freezing night temperatures. On some days, the temperature difference between daytime high and nighttime low can be 60 degrees, which was unfortunate for Arisi and Ch'askawani, working in their potato patch.

Already sweating profusely, Arisi stopped. Glancing over at Ch'askawani still mounding soil around the potato plants, he said, "Time for a break, my Beloved." Without responding, Ch'askawani followed Arisi to the edge of the field, where they each found a clump of feathergrass to sit on. The men were working in a patch of tubers just above and to the left of Ch'askawani's Compound.

Ch'askawani took the opportunity to share the details of the healing of Manqa's shoulder the previous night, to which Arisi responded, "Ch'askawani, you never cease to amaze."

"You might think it strange then," his Beloved replied, "to hear me say, I see myself as ordinary. What I do is natural, which is ordinary to me!"

"That makes sense; yet, people are not happy being who they are, ordinarily!

"Yes, because they are trying to be who they are not!" Ch'askawani stated.

Arisi laughingly said, "There's no trying to be who you are. It's natural."

Then Ch'askawani asked, "Can you authentically be who you are not?

"Wow, I never thought about that before. Strikes me as a long mountain trail to unhappiness."

"I agree," answered the Beloved young man. "To be ordinary means the uniqueness each one is born to express, which is a unique expression of the Great Spirit. That uniqueness makes the so-called ordinary extraordinary," Ch'askawani unveiled.

"I see your point. To be ordinary, or who you are, is effortless living," Arisi responded. "Trying to be extraordinary or who you are not but want to become for whatever reason is stressful because it requires adding unnecessary efforts. On the other hand, not striving to be different, an ordinary person is effortless and naturally different due to their uniqueness. Also, they can recognize the great variety of life, which is itself the extraordinary nature of the Great Spirit's attempt to know itself. When not spending life caught up with ideas of who one could be that they are not, one can finally view the magnificence of everything for what it is!"

"Well said, Arisi," Ch'askawani complimented, adding, "The ordinary forget they are ordinary, enabling them to live in peace. The ordinary are expressions of uniqueness. Everyone is born unique, or different, making us all the same!"

"The simple answer is humorously confusing, but true nonetheless," Arisi acknowledged.

"So let it be known, each of us is ordinary—uniquely so! You are you; I am me.

No one else for each of us to be," Ch'askawani concluded.

"That sums it up," Arisi replied, and both men began to laugh while standing up to return to work. At that moment, they heard a loud yawn from the direction of the Compound and looked to see who it was.

Manqa, coming out of one of the sleeping rooms of the Compound where he had slept the night at Ch'askawani's asking, so he could fully recover from the healing the night before, was yawning loudly and stretching his body. So much at peace, only the present moment filled his consciousness as he basked in the warmth of the sun. As Manqa lowered his arms, memories of the previous night flooded in. He grabbed his shoulder immediately. No pain. *I have no pain!* he thought to himself in great relief, then yelled it out loud for all to hear, "I have no pain, which indicates it's healed!"

Smiling at Arisi, Ch'askawani said, "I am going to go down and talk with Manqa. He seems to be a new man. I'll be back in a little while."

Arisi silently replied, nodding his head.

As he approached Manqa, standing still with his eyes closed, absorbing the sun's warmth, Ch'askawani saw a changed person from the night before. "Manqa, how are you feeling?" he asked.

Manqa opened his eyes and, seeing Ch'askawani, smiled and replied, "I feel great!" There was a new pronounced enthusiasm in his voice.

"I am so happy for you," Ch'askawani said, delighted. "I want to do one final check to ensure the healing was a success."

"No question about it being a success. I have no pain, and my body feels like new," Manqa replied confidently.

"Good, just come with me."

Manqa obediently followed Ch'askawani a short distance to a cluster of three old trees. One of the trees had a long horizontal branch. The seasoned healer knew the limb was about the length of Manqa's head, higher than Manqa could reach with his arms and hands fully extended upward. "I want you to jump up and grab hold of that branch above us and hang for a little while," Ch'askawani instructed.

"I don't think I want to do that yet," Manqa expressed hesitantly. The possibility of excruciating pain unnerved him.

"You need total confidence that your body healed, or you will continually favor that arm which will weaken the muscles in that shoulder and arm," Ch'askawani explained.

"I understand, but I am not ready to test my shoulder," Manqa said, quietly protesting.

"OK, then I want you to stand on top of this log next to where you are standing, which will allow you to grab hold of the branch and test your grip and arm strength," Ch'askawani instructed.

He was not seeing it as putting stress on his shoulder, so Manqa did as asked, stepping on top of the short log and grasping the branch.

"How does that feel?"

"Comfortable. No Strain, no pain."

"Good," Ch'askawani said as he walked behind Manqa and kicked the log out from under him. Manqa quickly grasped the branch tightly to avoid falling. His entire body weight was supported unexpectedly by his arms hanging on the limb. He was surprised.

"Just hang there until I count to 30," Ch'askawani requested. After the count ended, "You can release your grip now. The healing was a success."

Dropping to the ground, Manqa said, "I got angry because you tricked me, but when I realized that I had passed the true test without pain, it made me smile. Thank you. Thank you so much."

"Thank you for having faith I could heal your body."

"But it seems that more than I expected has happened," Manqa admitted.

"Here you are, as I suspected." The words turned the heads of both Ch'askawani and Manqa, who were both surprised to hear Waywa approaching.

"I woke up a short time ago with a splitting headache. When I finally recalled some of what happened last night, you weren't in the house, so I decided the first place to look was the last place I saw you, and here you are," Waywa explained, then asked, "What happened after I left? You look fine now."

"I had broken my shoulder bone. Thanks to Ch'askawani, it is now completely healed. Like new," Manqa announced.

Waywa looked at Ch'askawani with a surprised look on his face and said, "You healed a broken bone!"

"Ch'askawani healed not only the broken shoulder bone, but also the intense heat he generated cleansed my alcohol addiction, giving me a new life," Manqa added with pride, slapping Ch'askawani on the back. He put his arm around Ch'askawani as a gesture of genuine appreciation and turned his head to look at Waywa and smiled.

"You are most fortunate," Waywa admitted in a tone of sarcasm.

There was an air of jealousy in Waywa that Ch'askawani was able to detect, a lover's jealousy that misinterpreted Manqa's gesture of appreciation as something other than it was.

Ch'askawani looked at Waywa's tired face and his unkempt appearance, and smelled the odor of rancid body oil in his dirty clothes. Manqa, standing beside him, had a similar appearance, but he no longer carried an alcoholic's smell, and his attitude reflected an aliveness and enthusiasm foreign to Waywa. Ch'askawani knew Manqa's healing had purified his body from its alcohol dependency, which Ch'askawani intended, and such a cure carried far-reaching implications, including habit patterns and relationships. Waywa already had a sense of this, it seemed.

Staring at Manqa as he smiled, Waywa began to feel discomfort and thought to himself, *Manqa shows a change in attitude I didn't expect. His excitement could be relief from what must have been unbearable pain. Maybe this healing has done more than I realize. Perhaps it has taken Manqa from me.* First, there was a surge of fear, then anger. *I must get Manqa away from Ch'askawani's influence.* These thoughts prompted Waywa to suggest, "What do you say we go to the house? Maybe a drink to celebrate your full recovery?"

"No," Manqa responded to Waywa's surprise, "I am going to take a walk in the mountains alone. So many years have passed since I have taken in the natural beauty of this land. I'll see you back at the house later." Then Manqa turned to Ch'askawani and expressed a flow of gratitude, "I'll never be able to thank you enough for what you've done for me. I'm not sure I recognize the full extent of it yet, but time will tell. So, I'm off for a walk on this perfect sunny day." Having expressed those words, Manqa turned and walked off without further comment to Waywa.

Waywa stood silently, a bit surprised and a bit disturbed.

Ch'askawani stared at Waywa and watched his face take on a mad-dog look. Then, in anger, he said to Ch'askawani, "What have you done to my Manqa? What have you done to him?"

There was no immediate response from Ch'askawani; he only stared at Waywa, which was awkward for Waywa, who was used to aggression as a response to his anger.

The Precious One knew there would be no period of rehabilitation for Manqa. Manqa was healed, mind and body. His challenge would be determining who among the people would be against his new state of being, and who would accept him as a changed man. Ch'askawani also knew Manqa's homosexual interests complicated his situation. Waywa would have difficulty releasing his attachment to Manqa, even though Manqa would have far less of a problem releasing Waywa.

Ch'askawani was aware Waywa's anger was only the tip of a mountain ready to blow off and said to him, "Waywa, I understand how you feel..."

"How would you know how I feel?" Waywa interrupted bitterly.

"We all lose people to change. Some people change faster or slower than others. Others change in a different direction than the one we take. In any case, the change reflects expansion. A person can initiate change, which will be for the betterment of all, even though it doesn't appear so immediately—one of the ironies in a perfect world. You don't have to like the change that confronts you. Yet understand, it's easier to move on with your life when you accept that change is happening, rather than resisting it. The change for one is a change for all as we are all in this together...."

"Please, spare me!" Waywa shouted, "I don't need nor want your words! Isn't your point that I don't live up to your standard?"

"No, Beloved Waywa, that is not the point at all. Because you can't accept yourself, you think other people don't get you!" Ch'askawani fired back, "You are projecting your feelings on me and everyone else in the village. Love accepts all as they are; that alone changes a person. That's what you don't seem to grasp. The one creating the problem in your life is not me, Manqa, or the other villagers. It's you!

"If you would just be happy with your homosexual desires, neither you nor the others in the Gang of Four would feel and act like outcasts. None of the villagers have cast you out. Nor have I. You and the other three have done that to yourselves. Not willing to accept responsibility for your life choices and actions, you blame others for your group's decision to isolate yourselves.

"You don't love yourself, Waywa, because you see yourself as different. Yet are we not all different? It's the misperception of your uniqueness and everyone else's uniqueness. We're unique, not like anyone else. Tradition has told you since youth to think and act like others. That's the means by which you control yourself, by believing what tradition has indicated is acceptable behavior. You've been independent enough not to buy into that totally and have followed your feelings. But you've judged yourself and the others who are like you as wrong; otherwise, you, Manqa, Yanamayu, and Kichka would never have isolated yourselves from the other villagers all these years. Being who you are is a good thing. The Great Spirit sees that as being authentic and natural. You are here to show others not everyone's the same. That's not a bad thing; that's a reflection of how life is. You have shown no intent to harm others. Instead, you hurt yourself as punishment for the wrong YOU THINK YOU ARE DOING, then blame your actions on others' non-acceptance of you when it's only your own projection.

"You fail to enlighten others about your differences. Your failure to talk to others about homosexuality means you are making your desires secretive and unacceptable, from your point of view. You are terrorizing yourself; no one else is doing it to you. This failure to accept yourselves has taken all four men down a destructive path. You are trying to do away with your unhappiness imagining it was caused by others, when what's happening is that you and the other three men have been using your power against yourselves! Can you see this, Waywa?"

The man stood speechless; disappointment was written large on Waywa's face as Ch'askawani observed. Ch'askawani had bowled him over with the truth and could feel Waywa's suffering. Life would never be the same.

Waywa finally spoke. "The truth is so hard to accept and equally hard to deny. There are difficulties ahead for me. I don't want to blame you or Manqa, but I want to pin the blame on someone, and it hurts to think it's me. The fact is, I have failed to take responsibility for what I have become."

"Yes, but in claiming you didn't take responsibility, you are taking responsibility at this moment," Ch'askawani said in a consoling manner. "Sometimes people hide in what they think about themselves, or in wondering what others think of them."

"I admit I have done that. Being an alcoholic was easier than accepting the label of homosexual because I thought the latter label would isolate me. But, as it turned out, I chose not to accept myself for who I am when that pressure came from my thoughts projected on others! And it isolated me too. That led to reckless, uncontrolled drinking, frequent excuses, blaming others, and a constant focus on alcohol. I certainly have not felt good about myself for years. I have been tense, impatient, easily agitated, secretive, and defensive."

While listening, Ch'askawani thought, *this confession is what he needed. It's him telling himself how he has been. But if a sincere change occurs, there'll be a concession in his confession.*

"I cannot continue to be an alcoholic," Waywa went on to say. "I want to be refreshed, to feel as Manqa appeared to feel today. I want to be alive again!"

There it is, Ch'askawani thought, *he's giving up a life of an alcoholic to be in harmony with a desire to renew himself.*

Then Waywa suddenly blurted out, "I need a drink so bad right now!" and began crying.

Ch'askawani felt Waywa's insecurity, hugged him tightly, and let Waywa's tears fall on his shoulder, knowing full well that empathy and compassion healed. So, he allowed Waywa's tears to continue until done.

But Waywa's thought patterns, not the outside world, affected him. He had created a different body with specific chemical reactions corresponding to these thought patterns. To give up this self-destruction would be as if he had been born again in this life.

Waywa's tearful episode subsided, and Ch'askawani released him. As he sniffled, Waywa said, "Thank you for accepting who I am. I appreciate you not judging me. That alone has made me feel better."

"Love does not judge; it is a supportive hand when needed," Ch'askawani answered. "Here is where this matter gets confusing. You feel you have been irresponsible as the cause of what happened to you. Am I right?"

"Yes, but I will start taking responsibility for myself," Waywa insisted.

"Just a moment," Ch'askawani cautioned, "How can you be responsible when you don't act but react to situations occurring? Again, reactions are the ideas you have learned. Reacting is a matter of a reflex of habit, particularly the habit of identifying yourself as 'me.' You probably think you 'live' your life. Still, each life is part of the total movement of the entire physical creation. Experiencing you is the One, the Great Spirit of Consciousness who never sees itself, only what it witnesses, and who is responsible for this total manifestation to know itself more fully."

"Then how am I supposed to heal myself from alcohol abuse?" Waywa inquired in a tone of desperation.

"Beloved Waywa, a habit has brought you to this point. How you respond to the changes around you will stimulate other habits. You are not doing anything like the person called Waywa. You are formless Great Spirit of Consciousness watching all that happens. Yet, you think you are Waywa, a habit obstructing the realization of your identity—a non-being! So, what am I saying? Simply this— Don't do what you think you can do to heal. But you are to live naturally and spontaneously, without planning or any preconceived ideas. In short, cut off your head!" Ch'askawani advised.

"I take it you mean 'cut off my head' as don't allow the mind to interfere?" Waywa asked.

"Exactly. Without thinking, there'll be no idea of 'doing.' There will be physical reactions but not because you think you are doing something. You will see it all happening before you, but not by Waywa!" Ch'askawani indicated with confidence.

There was silence for a while. Ch'askawani could tell Waywa was digesting what was said. Waywa asked no questions for further clarification.

"Do you know yourself?" Ch'askawani asked.

"I think I do, as much as one can. Why are you asking?" Waywa asked, puzzled.

"What you think about yourself and what you know about yourself are not the same things. What you consider yourself is a fantasy. You use your imagination. And this fantasy is maintained by imagining what others think about you, which is your thoughts, not another's, or what you think of others. Both instances are cases of thinking, not knowing.

"Knowing is an expanding awareness coming from direct experience, either within or witnessing another. The resurrection of Miski is an example of observing a body dead for several days come back to life. Did this event not influence you?"

"Yes, but I have to admit I was still drunk and stood at the back of the gathering. So I didn't hear Miski."

"OK, that's understandable," Ch'askawani empathized. "Realize no one can take that direct experience from you, not even people who deny it happened because they weren't there to see it. Witnessing this is true knowing, as it expanded the observer's awareness of not only her but also the observer's.

"Different experiences suggest how different people are. That's important to know because life is that way. So, love yourself, no matter the circumstance, and learn to take care of yourself rather than abuse yourself. I will be talking about this tomorrow at the village gathering," Ch'askawani concluded as he thought to himself, *this is just the beginning of another course correction on an endless journey. The destination is knowing oneself.*

After Waywa left Ch'askawani's company, the wind beneath his wings, which allowed him to soar, suddenly stopped. The enthusiasm, insight, and momentum vanished as quickly as water poured on desert sand. Waywa had decided on a contemplative walk as Manqa had done and proceeded up the mountain slope above the village. As he continued past the last fields, his breathing was labored, and he felt faint. To recover, he sat down, with his knees bent and legs against his chest, laid his forearms across the top of the kneecaps, and rested his forehead on his arms with his eyes closed. Not only was he physically tired, but mentally exhausted, thinking to himself, *does fatigue make cowards as it does me?*

Waywa sat quietly in this posture. Occasionally words from the conversation with Ch'askawani would be remembered and lift his sinking mood.

You are terrorizing yourself; no one else is doing it to you

We're made unique

You have judged yourself as wrong; otherwise, you wouldn't have isolated yourself all those years.

You are here to show others not everyone is the same

I don't want to blame you or Manqa, but I want to pin the blame on some, and it hurts to think it's me

I failed to take responsibility for what I have become

Being an alcoholic was effortless compared to accepting the label of homosexual

I can't continue to be an alcoholic

I want to be alive again

Thank you for getting me

What you think of yourself is a fantasy

How different people are

Life is that way

Take care of yourself first

You are not the doer

Don't allow thinking to interfere

He thought to himself, *these words are one thing, but I don't smell the fresh air like Manqa would. Oozing out of my body pores is a fluid with a foul smell. As it evaporates, it encircles me with a trans-parent vapor cloud. I stink. The smell is repulsive, and I detest my-self for allowing this to happen.*

Possibly the change, he sensed, *I desperately wish for, is like this long uphill walk I've started. Maybe it is beyond me, both physically and mentally?* Waywa had begun to doubt. *Where has my courage gone?* He wondered. *I have caused an unpleasantly tricky situation. I must adjust to the changes other people like Manqa are making. I thought I was in control of myself, but Ch'askawani pointed out no one was! I must accept that change is inevitable. Change itself doesn't sound threatening. It's WHAT must change—ME—that does.*

Suddenly, a voice said: "What's the matter with you?" The deep guttural tone was unmistakable, harsh, and throaty. It was Guari. Absorbed in his thoughts, Waywa never heard Guari's approach. Nor did he lift his head immediately to acknowledge Guari; in-stead he thought, *I wonder what he wants? He's the pushy sort. Insensitive, manipulative, forceful, and intimidating. I* don't *feel like talking to him.*

Then, as if providing Waywa's point, Guari said, "You can't speak? Got no tongue, or are you drunk as usual?"

Waywa was not in the mood. He raised his head, glared at Guari's big round face, and said, "You must have been going someplace before you stopped to bother me."

"Aren't we sensitive?" was Guari's quick sarcastic retort.

Waywa smiled, tightening his lips in a sarcastic expression then asked, "Guari, what are you and Atoc doing in Sonqollaqta anyway? You two are not farmers. What are you up to?"

"If you really want to," Guari answered, "The Inca Empire is starting to expand. Our plan in coming here is to work our way into positions of authority. We are aware of the Inca tactics toward those they intend to conquer, which begins with diplomatic offers of trade, monetary rewards, high-ranking jobs, and influential marriages. Atoc and I want to be in positions to receive these offerings. The only obstacle in our way is the independent-minded Ch'askawani."

"You must be joking, or just foolish," Waywa grimly mocking Guari.

As if unaffected, Guari replied, "Just thought you and your buddies would like to know Atoc and I have planned to get rid of Ch'askawani. Atoc and I will be on an extended visit to Qosqo, so we won't be around when it happens. This way, we won't be accused of foul play."

"Accused? Accused of what?" Waywa asked. "Are you going to kill him?"

"How would I know? I won't be here," Guari replied with a devious grin, adding, "You boys won't have to worry about changing your lives to please others in the village. This village will become part of the Inca Empire, and you can help collect tribute for the Empire from the other villagers and rake-off as much as we want for ourselves. So, we'll live fat and happy."

Displeased, Waywa looked at Guari's enormous belly and responded, "Looks like you have accomplished half of your purpose already," then laughed.

"You little worm," Guari shouted, outraged, "I should beat you to death right here! No witnesses. No one would know."

"I would!" The unexpected voice came from behind Guari, who spun around quickly to determine who it was.

"Oh, it's you, Manqa. What are you up to?" Guari said in a completely calm voice.

"You were threatening Waywa. Why?" Manqa asked.

"I was kidding around. I was telling Waywa my prediction concerning Ch'askawani's demise."

Immediately Manqa jumped in, "So you can propel yourself into a seat of power and control the lives of the villagers. Ch'askawani wants to free us; you want to enslave us. The difference is day and night. Any plan you have to destroy another will only lead to the destruction of the destroyer."

"Do you take me to be a fool, Manqa?" Guari protested. "There will be no tracks to cover. I am merely foretelling or predicting what is to come. It's a premonition not unlike our dear Ch'askawani's."

"Sounds like a plot to me!" Waywa offered with a suspicious glare at Guari.

Then Manqa spoke again, "Alcohol alters people's minds. But some are in altered states due to a thirst for power. Waywa and I are the former, you, the latter. We may destroy our bodies. That's our own business. But power involves other people. So, your thirst for power is bound to lead to the opposite result for you, Guari. Most of the villagers don't like you or Atoc!"

"Words of no importance from a man who has no standing in the village beyond the label of village drunk," Guari taunted Manqa without knowing of his complete healing from alcohol. Guari added, "Well, I have to go. I just hope you two don't end up on the wrong side. See you later."

Guari sauntered off across the open terrain toward the village.

Waywa and Manqa watched Guari until he was out of hearing range. Then Manqa looked at Waywa, "This guy is trouble."

"I am not sure we can take him seriously," Waywa replied.

"I am not sure we shouldn't take him seriously!" Manqa insisted, then said, "How did you wind up in a conversation with him out here anyway?"

"After you departed on your walk this morning," Waywa explained, "Ch'askawani and I talked about the changes people go through and how the differences affect relationships. He talked about how your healing would affect me if I didn't change. He was very kind and understanding. I have never spent any time with him and only saw him through the lens of my insecurity. He helped me see what has happened to me, and that what will happen does not depend on anyone else but me. I am responsible for my life. I want to change, but it may take more from me than I must give. We shall see. For sure, I want to be free of this liquid monster that has consumed me as I have consumed it."

"I am happy to hear this. You are the love of my love," Manqa admitted. "That will not change, whether we live together or not, whether we are compatible or not. Where this relationship goes will depend on both of us interacting. But I will always love you.

"Today, I looked back on the years at the different subjects Ch'askawani talked about and, surprisingly, I remember quite a bit. However, today I understood the meaning of many of his words for the first time. Once, he told us to remove ideas we repeat as tradition, which we follow blindly. He emphasized we cannot remove ignorance of our true nature by acquiring knowledge. Because ignorance is the result of the ideas we have identified with traditionally. He has proceeded cautiously and yet boldly to guide all who would listen in such a way, so we think we find the answers ourselves.

"Ch'askawani told the villagers on more than one occasion, what prevents us from seeing who we truly are is a desire for something we don't have or to be someone we are not. Desire is only an obstacle. Even our desires to liberate ourselves from alcohol's bondage is an obstacle," Manqa explained.

"Why?" Waywa asked, puzzled as this desire was exactly his issue.

"Why? Because there has never been any bondage to be freed from," Manqa replied. We have both chosen by our thoughts and actions and chose differently from one moment to the next if aware of the power we hold. So, there is no desire from which to be freed. Bondage and freedom are both ideas used to keep the fantasy alive. Just as right and wrong, good or bad, happiness or sorrow are ideas we carry in our minds. Aren't we just pretending to be doers who THINK we are doing? We are witnesses to what's happening.

"Only ideas carry us to unhappiness and the desires of how to overcome it, which may only perpetuate it. Neither exists. They are only thoughts we identify as in our heads. We not only identify as thinking beings, but we also recognize ourselves as specific thoughts!

"On my walk today, I finally got it. By realizing I am not the body, revisiting the experience of Miski's return from the dead, I understand that I am not the doer. It appears the body is. But the doer is the enormous field of consciousness we call the Great Spirit when we are not identifying as the idea of the doer. Then I can see that I am just a witness when I dream. You and I and everyone else are the Great Spirit, the formless witness. It seems that is what Miski was alluding to!"

"Look, Manqa," Waywa said abruptly, "You have been healed from alcohol and can see clearly. I have not. I still have to contend with...."

"...**with identifying yourself as** an alcoholic?" Manqa replied, nipping Waywa's excuse in the bud. "What if you just observed unhappiness rather than being unhappy? Observed yourself in homosexual activity without calling it homosexuality? What if you just observed yourself, rather than judged and labeled yourself? Even desires are a way of identifying yourself as or as not something."

"I have to agree. I did feel the release of tension when I chose not to view myself as a label or judge that label," Waywa admitted.

"Yes, to say you are suffering is identifying **as if you are the idea of suffering**. But this is a use of words that distorts the true expression: I THINK I am suffering, rather than just accepting what is occurring at that moment. It's not experiencing the moment; it's experiencing thinking about the moment. Thinking is the altered state of consciousness Ch'askawani has been telling us over the years. You alter the Great Spirit of Consciousness by thinking you're the label Waywa. You are not aware of who you are; you identify with who you are not.

Thinking expands the altered state of thinking, not the moment of WHAT-IS. Are we living the story of the thoughts we are creating that explain each moment? Or are we experiencing each moment?"

"Wow, man, Ch'askawani would be proud of you. You have blown away the clouds of identification, and the sky is clear!" Waywa complimented, adding, "It just occurred to me, all I need to get through this recovery is a clear understanding of this life quite different from the ideas about this life, for me to have no judgments of myself based on ideas learned. But I recognize a relaxed acceptance of What-Is, free of doubt or opinion. Thank you, Manqa, my love, for reminding me in the clearest terms!"

Manqa chuckled, saying, "I wonder, do we find the answers by ourselves, or do we need a seed planted in us? Anyway, doesn't this new view of reality allow everything to be OK? To have faith that there's more to life, much more than thoughts about life?"

"Yes, you are right. Right now, I am thinking something about Miski's experience, as if some wires in my brain are reconnecting. I see something that I was not able to see back then. Wasn't one of the implications of Miski's experience that 'me' cannot be different from 'you' without a body? Is it not the Great Spirit returning to itself? Are fear and conflict absent? I missed that possibility before when still drunk, I heard her speak about her experience. I could greatly value that experience **now**, but not then. You've helped me see I can end desires and feel the peace of existing without identifying as anything. What would I be other than I AM THAT I AM! I cannot believe I am realizing the value of her experience more than twenty years after it happened."

"You are incredible, and who isn't," Manqa said without the intent of flattery. "The presence of Ch'askawani is showing you, me, and the villagers who are open to the possibility, life being created anew. Think about this for a moment, dear Waywa.

"The answers to survival have been worked out by our ancestors thousands of years ago, which created a viable survival template to replicate for all of us who came later. We call tradition this path of survival shown to generations of Quechuan youth starting at a very young age. An ordinary life, predictable from birth to death, resulted. Ch'askawani shows us the possibility of making everyday life extraordinary by expanding our awareness of our true nature. While enabling us to survive and thrive materially, tradition has limited our view of life.

"The boredom and monotony of repetition and the destructive adaptations that come with it, such as alcoholism, violence, and abuse, can be replaced by a vision extending each of us beyond this earthly confinement. Maybe this was the original intention of the Ch'usaq Pacha in gifting Ch'askawani to us those many years ago. Wouldn't it be a kick if our true home is in the stars too?"

6

S age-like, Ch'askawani strolled on a well-worn village path, passed the scattered houses eastward, bound to the meeting place.

He felt the air more invigorating than usual, the sky cloudier than expected for the dry season, the leaves on the trees starting to change color. *Signs of the rainy season approaching,* Ch'askawani thought, *today's meeting will most likely be the last before the rains come.* Stopping briefly to gaze at the white billowy clouds rolling in waves, he immediately began unexpectedly reflecting on his life.

A mere fifty years have passed since my arrival here on a starship. On my home planet, beings typically live 800-1,000 years. I'm just getting started on my journey here. So many remarkable and wondrous healings have occurred before me, and inspiring talks have come from my lips. Yet, there is something not quite right here, I am sensing. There is a mutual rising on this planet. There's light and there's darkness coursing through the hearts and minds of people, as day and night. While I am cosmic light, I feel 'darkness' is becoming more active here, and I am its target... .

"Hey, blue eyes!" A familiar voice interrupted. He turned to one side and saw her.

"Yeah, blue eyes! How is Ru'qu today?"

"I am fine," was her polite reply.

As each caught the gaze of the other, both were mesmerized by the blue eyes each saw. Both were the only ones with blue eyes in a community of brown eyes. They were as if seeing each other for the first time, again.

"We have spent no time alone," Ru'qu admitted.

"An accurate observation. Neither of us has taken the time to get to know the other, yet we share the same mother and father. How strange is that? We need to change this situation and do it soon," Ch'askawani answered, drawn suddenly to her as if under a spell.

"I would like that very much," Ru'qu replied, then added, "Strangely, you seem so familiar to me as if we have been together before."

"We have," Ch'askawani answered bluntly, deciding she ought to know about her past.

"How is that possible?" Ru'qu inquired.

"You, as I have informed so many before, are a spirit. You were a woman named Miski, formerly a resident of the village. She dropped her body before you were born," Ch'askawani said.

"Wow, the woman who returned from the dead and was able to live to a ripe old age. I am that woman?" Ru'qu raised her eyebrows in surprise.

Ch'askawani nodded affirmatively. Then she added, as a flirting comment, "Just as we've been together before, and we are here now!"

"Let's walk together to the gathering and talk along the way about getting together soon," Ch'askawani responded, smiling.

Surprising herself and Ch'askawani, Ru'qu slipped her arm around his and said, "Let's go!"

After a brief hesitation, he said, smiling, "Alright, let's go!" Both dashed down the path for a distance, then abruptly stopped, laughing, and giggling like two kids over their spontaneous action. Then, after catching their breath, they proceeded at a more casual pace.

Approaching the gathering place, the two could hear the crowd's murmurs and noticed most of the villagers were already seated. A ray of sunlight fell on Ru'qu's face, the brightness causing her to blink and look up. The heavy cloud cover was quickly thinning, and the sun's rays began to bathe the landscape in light as she scanned the villagers for Kuychi and Arisi, who promised to save her a place to sit. She caught sight of them waving at her and moved in their direction.

As more villagers saw Ch'askawani standing in position, a hush slowly spread over the crowd, which was his cue to begin. "Dear Beloveds, thank you for coming today and for inspiring me to inspire you more.

"No runakuna (people) live more naturally than the Quechua runakuna, farming the land and caring for the animals, living in harmony with the landscape and the weather. As if by magic, you turn dirt into food, make food into flesh and bones, designate many spaces on the terrain as sacred, and make offerings to the guardian spirits. Even the mountains are holy places based on the belief that our ancestors arose from the land. In honor of this belief, offerings and sacrifices return wealth from the ground. This harmonious interaction with the sacred land is essential. But this is not a complete view, nor will ever be until you look at yourselves as sacred too.

"The greatest act of making life sacred is making the body in which each of you live a house of worship. The accumulation of material possessions is not essential, nor will it make a fundamental difference in your life. However, being in a sacred space will make a difference beyond what you think is possible. Taking this view is the only way to be in a sacred space every moment of your life. You can choose to accept this existence as initially intended, as sacred. The choice is always yours. Choosing is your freedom from bondage to this land. If you continue to follow tradition and refuse to acknowledge your power, your life will not be as valuable as it would be otherwise. Choosing enables you to make your life worthwhile, for you and all. At present, your choice is a curse. Life is exhausting, and you gain temporary distraction by drinking alcohol, and suffer from a cycle of domestic violence.

How sacred can this life be for you? Each of you is the presence of the Great Spirit in the mountains. But the mask of ideas you currently wear is the source of your limitations of who you are. Freedom is not freeing yourself from the control of others; it is freeing yourself from the ideas that bind you. The truth is, when you think someone has power over you, it is only your thoughts that confine you to that possibility."

Guari and Atoc, who were in the crowd, looked at each other. Then, finally, the big man leaned over to the ear of Atoc and whispered, "I am not liking what I am hearing. We cannot control independent-minded people."

"Authentic and ordinary runa (person) wants peace, love, to be left alone, and freedom to be himself or herself. Regular activities can be sacred if you give up identification as thoughts, feelings, desires, fears, and regrets. Without judgment, you can see others as a unique expression of the Great Spirit, not as an enemy or a foe. Without identifying with thoughts, feelings, desires, fears, or regrets, who could be hurt, injured, or insulted?

"If you observe your thoughts, feelings, desires, and fears without acting on them, only witness your regrets without working on them, you allow the divine you are to transform them into their succeeding highest form, which is eternal light. But the overwhelming tendency is to weave these thoughts, feelings, desires, fears, and regrets into the fabric of your identity, into your storyline. You think these things are your life. They are not.

"You are like a tunnel of light. Everything passes through you to be acknowledged and released, returned to the source of its origin, back into the wholeness, purity, and perfection of the Great Spirit. That is, of course, when you don't identify as them. But how many times do you say to yourself or someone else,

'I am angry.'

'I am sad.'

'I am afraid.'

'I feel hurt.'

"I am unhappy'.

Or 'I am stupid for thinking this.'

'I am difficult to deal with.'

'I feel unsafe.'

'I want a beautiful wife or handsome husband.'

"I want more power.'

'I fear him.'

'I fear them.'

'I am sorry for what I did to you.'

'I regret not telling that person how I felt about her or him.'

"These are lines we identify as and create storylines of larger stories. For example, 'I am unhappy because....' To witness these ideas, feelings, desires, fears, and regrets, without claiming to own them or identify as them is to be free of them.

"So much of what we say to ourselves becomes a curse, negative comments which lead to thinking and feeling we are unworthy, unable, and powerless. And, what you express negatively about someone else, your ears hear, as if you're talking to yourself. When you think thoughts about another person, you are not thinking thoughts about them; you are thinking about **your ideas** about them. When talking about another, you're talking about **your thoughts and feelings** about another, not another. Even your description of another person is your idea of that person, not that person. That's why backbiting and gossiping are just about yourself, although you use someone else's name.

"Each of your bodies is a divine creation, created by the Great Spirit to know itself better. View the body from this unique perspective. Don't harm it—not yours or another's. Life becomes a sacred wholeness or holiness when you fully respect your body, yourself, and everything around you.

"I'd like to add to something I said earlier. I mentioned that thoughts, feelings, desires, fears, and regrets are released through each of you and returned to the purity of the Great Spirit IF you don't identify as them but observe their occurrence. Since each of you is the Great Spirit, you will see these expressions transformed in your lives. You'll see a thorough or dramatic change in the form, appearance, or character of your lives by transforming. Purification is that change. I'll mention the impure and the pure forms they change into, giving you the means of detecting and feeling change when it occurs. Here's what to look for:

Hate transforms into love.

Selfishness transforms into helpfulness and charity.

Cruelty transforms into mercy.

Despair transforms into hope.

Mistrust transforms into faith.

Pride transforms into humility.

Indifference transforms into compassion.

Un-discipline transforms into self-control.

Injustice transforms into justice.

Impatience transforms into patience.

Discord transforms into concord, or harmony between people.

"These, my Beloveds, are the highest strivings to reach for in this life or any life. These achievements bring glory in the stars to the Quechuan homeland.

"The more the body's senses of touch, seeing, hearing, pick up these changes in the environment, the more aware you will be that change is occurring.

"When you hear more praise, encouragement, compliments, your self-worth increases, which means that you'll be more willing you'll be to listen to another. The greater self-worth is, the more empowered and more capable you become. As a result, you are more willing to assert yourself to help others, be generous, and care for others.

"The more often you see helping, see acts of kindness and generosity, see compassion, see courage, see healing, see hugging, see affection, see gestures of appreciation, you see your World changing for the better."

"Does this make sense to you?"

Ch'askawani scanned the faces at the gathering, and he saw many nodding their heads, affirming what he had said.

"Another point that ties in here needs to be understood. So many are struggling to find happiness when happiness is your natural state. You are unconditionally happy. That means you don't require anything or anyone as a condition for being happy. Unhappiness comes, as you might suspect, if you have been listening to, or have, thoughts, feelings, desires, fears, and regrets. For example, when sadness arises in you, acknowledge it and don't identify as it. You don't say, 'I am sad.' That's identifying as it. Instead, you say, 'sadness has arisen in me. I feel it.' Realize how it makes you feel, sit with it, but don't act on it. Then say, 'I release this feeling back to the source of its origin, the purity, wholeness, and perfection of the Great Spirit from which it came.'"

"Here again, you can detect the sources of unhappiness. So, if you are unhappy, you identify as some thought, feeling, desire, fear, or regret. It's that simple.

"Let's consider desires. These are usually items or people you want but don't have in your life. To be constantly wanting something or someone is to be constantly unfulfilled. How does that make you feel? Unhappy? Not only that, but you are thinking about it frequently, thinking about something not carried out or brought to completion. You think you are incomplete, and you feel unsatisfied. This example shows desires, and also involves thoughts and feelings and fears and regrets.

"The easy way to overcome the unfulfillment of desires is to look at them differently. Instead of viewing a desire as something or someone you want but don't have, see a desire as what you do have. You can say to yourself, 'I desire the spouse I have, the child or children I have. I desire the house I have; I desire the food I have available to eat; I desire doing what I am doing; I desire the life I have. In other words, abide with what you have, as if it is what you want.

"To see yourself this way is to feel fulfilled by your life circumstances, instead of thinking something is missing. Again, each person is only unhappy because they think, feel, desire, fear, or regret.

"Please don't misunderstand. I am not saying, don't think, don't feel, don't desire, don't fear, or don't regret. These impressions cannot be released if you deny them. You must acknowledge and accept them. The point is not to make a story out of the moment, which carries over into many moments after. That's living in the past, reliving past impressions.

"Just remember the life force goes where attention goes. Stop paying attention to an impression, and it will die a natural death. Instead, give full attention to what is arising at each moment, then release it from your focus. Be in the moment that is happening, not a past or a future moment.

"Not identifying as thoughts, feelings, desires, fears, or regrets is the remedy for the unhappiness you feel. You limit yourself by repeating these impressions. Without 'identifying as', there's no confinement, no limitation. You are free.

"By not 'identifying as' the Great Spirit uses its attention to expand immeasurably, realizing it is not an individual body, it is not a single expression, but all expressions. It is endless in expressing itself. When this occurs, you do not love others, you'll enjoy BEING others! I am sure this sounds odd, but this is true bliss!

"What you realize in this World is the appearance of the Great Spirit, not something separately projected by the Great Spirit. So, the appropriate question is, what do I have to do with thoughts, feelings, desires, fears, and regrets when I am the Great Spirit?

"The Great Spirit is self-aware. It knows it exists. It is the 'I AM.' However, the Great Spirit only knew itself as a void, as emptiness, for an unknown duration. Then came the question, 'I am, but who? Who am I? The question unleashed the zest to know itself. The Great Spirit as a creative force exploded. All of existence that came about was only the Great Spirit's innocent attempt to understand itself. Not only did it create everything and everyone, but it also jumped into its Creation to experience itself as everything and everyone. The Great Spirit is ONE as ALL. You are beyond what you think and can imagine.

"So, the Great Spirit is all there is, watching itself. It is alone or all-one. There is no crowd watching.

"If what I have said is confusing to many of you, it's ok. I will explain the most important part in simplest terms using a visual example, making it easier to understand and remember."

Ch'askawani held up his right hand and said, "I want everyone to look at your right hand. Touch the first finger to the thumb several times, like this."

Extending his right arm skyward, he touches his first finger and thumb several times. "Think of this action as interacting with someone, anyone. If you look at the finger and thumb, you see that they are connected, the same hand. While you and the other person appear to be interacting, both are only on the one hand. The Great Spirit is interacting with itself!

"Take each finger as the Great Spirit expanding along different lines of development yet maintaining its ability to interact with each unique expression of itself.

"In this physical World, we see each finger as a body, but the Great Spirit you are is the invisible force animating each body. The Great Spirit is an all-present life force giving life to forms that appear separate and identify with the idea of being separate. The primary issue is 'identifying as.' First, identify as an individual and then further as thoughts, feelings, desires, fears, and regrets. It is not a case of losing yourself. You never lose what you are. You only get lost in thoughts, feelings, desires, fears, and regrets you 'identify as'."

Ch'askawani stopped, looked up at the blue sky with only a few clouds drifting by and the sun shining brightly, then instructed, "Would you all please stand up."

Once all were standing, he continued, "If you look down at your feet, you see your shadow on the ground. The shadow represents the body, and you, the observer, are the Great Spirit for our purpose. The question to you is, can the 'shadow body' do anything to you? Can it move you? Can it make you raise your arm?"

Some of the villagers looked confused while others yelled, "No!"

"Of course not," Ch'askawani concurred, adding, "The shadow representing the body cannot move you. It cannot act. You are the source of all the body's movements. You move the body. And further, can the body learn anything? Can it solve problems? Can it figure out solutions?"

Again, the answer came back, "No," but more responded this time.

"Correct, this is the nature of physical existence. You, the Great Spirit, operate the physical body. You are the source of its actions. You are the source of actions in all bodies!" Ch'askawani affirmed,

"Please understand, I am explaining what is not understood through examples that are understood. No mind is too tiny for expanded perception. Direct experience is the most reliable indicator.

"Messages of an expanded look at reality are Miski's return from the dead, sight returned to Catequil, and Manqa's broken shoulder bone instantly healed. If open to these messages, a reality beyond our thoughts, feelings, desires, fears, and regrets appears.

"When you continue to cling to the past, you block yourself from expanding yourself. Those who have experienced these fantastic events or witnessed them become messengers of their expansion."

Unexpectedly, Waywa stood. He appeared tired; his face replete with wrinkles from dehydration from years of drunkenness. He looked beyond his years. To the surprise of many, he asked, "Ch'askawani, what hope is there for those of us who cannot live without drinking our lives away?"

"Waywa," Ch'askawani responded, "thank you for having the courage to ask such a question. Here is an insight about drinking as it relates to thinking. While a drinker is aware that constant drinking leads to an altered state of awareness, affecting hearing, seeing, touch, balance, and movement, most thinkers are in an altered state without realizing it.

"Neither excessive drinking nor habitual thinking enables a person to see reality beyond the sensations experienced, which are only ideas of what's happening. Furthermore, over-thinking, like worrying, may well be the cause of excessive drinking! Worrying about what others may think of you is being afraid of a situation that only exists in your imagination. Worrying may even be the source of a desire to escape the boredom and monotony of routine habits. Is life difficult? Or is it the way it is perceived? If you cannot view the World differently, is that the World's problem? Or the viewer's problem? How can you blame life for decisions you've made, or for consequences of your thoughts and actions you don't like?

"The drinker is trapped by the habit of drinking as well as the pattern of what he is drinking. So too, the thinker is confined by the habit of thinking and the repetitive pattern of what he's thinking! Repetition of thoughts, or patterns formed, confines your attention, and blocks the expansion of existence.

"Stop identifying as a particular thought, feeling, desire, fear, or regret. When you change your perspective on what you are looking at, you change what you see. The situation appears to change, but it is your view of it that is changing. And that's because all is in the eyes of the observer. What is observed or seen is determined by the seer's point of view.

"When you open to what is happening, not ideas of what's happening, all is possible. As I have said already, withdraw your energy. What has no life force ceases. That applies to the body if you leave it permanently. It applies to thoughts you leave, feelings you leave, desires you leave, and regrets you leave. Do you see, when you can let things go, you change?

"Freedom is only possible within. Here's an important realization to keep in mind: Where your attention goes, your energy goes. If you confine your attention to thoughts you've been taught, you confine your energy too. You're bound by habitual thoughts, feelings, desires, fears, and regrets.

"If you're free to change perspectives, the World outside cannot confine or hold you to anything for very long. Change is often spontaneous and natural, but blocked by the thoughts, feelings, desires, fears, and regrets you're conditioned to repeat. They keep you the same. If you can release this conditioning, everything around you will change because everything in you has changed.

"What you are is more than what you tell yourself. Instead of thinking you know who you are, ask what the Great Spirit asked: 'Who am I?' The only hint I can give you is you're not a thought, a feeling, a desire, a fear, or a regret. These you experience, but who is the experiencer? The experiencer is more important than the experience because they can change what's happening. Don't be lost in the impression of thinking, feeling, desiring, fearing, or regretting, which have become the basis for your actions.

"Waywa, I hope this answered your question. The answer was a little long winded," Ch'askawani concluded.

"Yes, you answered it and added much more valuable information to contemplate. Thank you," Waywa, replied, "I have another question. Tradition results in all of us being so much alike. You mentioned tradition. Is that it?

"Good question, Waywa," Ch'askawani replied. "The quick answer is survival. As I indicated, tradition responded to how to survive. Nothing is possible if one does not survive. But the answer is incomplete.

The answers to your survival were worked out thousands of years earlier by your ancestors, which explains why our lifestyle has remained almost unchanged over that period. The Quechuan tradition is a proven template for not how to survive, but how to thrive. The basis of life has come from our own hands living as farmers, cultivating the land, and as herders, raising livestock to provide the necessities of survival: Food, clothing, and shelter.

"The Quechuan agrarian way of life enabled our ancestors to grow in numbers, supporting large numbers in the interior mountain valleys. Unfortunately, the numbers grew to the point where over-crowding and depletion of the soil occurred, which forced groups such as our relatives to split off and move, opening new areas to live, some less desirable than others.

"Settling on this high mountain land on the eastern slope where we are today was the choice of parents of many of you who are only the second generation in Sonqollaqta.

"Because of the harsher environmental conditions at this high al-titude, we've had a greater reliance on animal husbandry, raising llamas and alpacas and making goods to trade from their thick wool coats as well as providing a means of transporting goods and as a reliable food source.

"Because of our homeland's altitude, most of the rain falls on the mountainside well below us. This lack of rain means poor soil con-ditions, leading to stunted crops and lean harvests. But those who came before showed incredible ingenuity, extracting exceptional yields by preventing water from evaporating from the soil by simply planting and cultivation methods to limit exposure of the subsoil, eliminating moisture evaporation. They were also smart enough to select and nurture crops that were most resistant to frost damage and thrive in poor soil.

"In addition, they created methods of food preservation such as freeze-drying papas and meat, which took advantage of the freezing nights and warm days. Your continued resourcefulness is comprehending what conditions confronted you and adjusting to those conditions in the most remarkable ways. This cleverness applied to making clothing items resulted in items practical and beautifully made. Yet, this all relates to survival. But you must admit you approached it quite creatively. You've shown once you can survive, you can create and perform spontaneously or without preparation. You have started to create music, dance, and verse. You are already finding the answer naturally, you are expanding! How far this expansion goes for each of you depends on the perspective each develops. So, everything is ok. Just keep expanding!

"Here is the significant difference in approaching life. What you do to survive is by intention. But to expand spiritually or into higher realms of existence doesn't require conscious effort. Such change is watching the release of all that you have learned. The observer does not think they are doing things, but observes things being done. You observe yourself and witness others, not to judge what is happening, but to eliminate the idea of being a doer. The doer identifies as thoughts, feelings, desires, fears, and regrets. The observer who just watches is not affiliated with anything, but observes the whole Design moving by his force. The Creator and the movement of Creation are the same. You cannot recognize one without the other. You cannot fully appreciate the movement of the cosmos without awareness of the Creator.

Apo jumped to his feet and asked, "I am confused. How is that possible, Ch'askawani? You have said that thoughts, feelings, desires, fears, and regrets block us from experiencing who we truly are. It doesn't seem very clear to me. How can the one who creates and experiences its Design do things which prevent it from understanding Itself? I don't understand!"

"I must state clearly; there is nothing wrong with identifying as thoughts, feelings, desires, fears, and regrets. However, identities help the Great Spirit realize '**who It is not**,' which is an inseparable aspect of expanding self-awareness.

"The situation would be the same as before Creation occurred, the Great Spirit knowing it exists but unaware of who it is. By creating, it knows it's the Source. By creating endless possibilities, it knows it is all-powerful. By jumping into its Creation, it experiences itself firsthand to be mindful of being all-knowing. By being itself in un-ending variety, it is all blissful, experiencing itself fully.

"Repetition may appear to be an exception to what I've just said, but, as I have said before, everything has value in this World, and so repetition has value as part of the perfection of existence. Its value is in showing each of us how repetition limits us! There is repetition, which is valuable such as eating, keeping the body alive; but there are repeated thoughts which are harmful, such as thinking you have the right to beat someone or abuse them. It is important to distinguish what serves the wellbeing of all from that which serves the interests of only a few.

"Apo, you have brought to light an interesting point. I appreciate you paying attention to what I've said. I see you understand much. There are two paths to expanding life. The short path and the long path. Suffering is a long path. But realize both paths lead you to who you truly are. Allow me an illustration."

Ch'askawani turned in the direction of Arisi and asked, "Arisi, could you please bring me the bow and arrow?"

Arisi stood and walked the two items to Ch'askawani as the speaker further explained, "I have asked Arisi to bring to me a bow and arrow he acquired in the Lowlands, used by the people in the jungle for hunting. The bow and arrow show the simple mechanism of Creation. I want to show you how identification and repetition, which appear to block expanded awareness, can bring it about. Remember, everything in Creation has value, even the long path, because it gets you to where you want to go!"

Arisi handed the bow and arrow to Ch'askawani and returned to his seat. "Thank you, Arisi."

"Now," Ch'askawani began his instruction, "Holding the bow, I pull back the string. The further I pull it back, the faster and farther the arrow will fly forward. Moving forward reflects your expansion; the backward direction of the arrow shows more and more tension or pressure we call suffering. So, the longer you identify with thoughts, feelings, desires, fears, and regrets, the more suffering occurs. When you reach the point when suffering is too much, you let go. The example shows, the greater the suffering, the further you propel yourself spiritually when you finally let go of ideas that define you.

"This example should show you whatever you think is working against your expansion is, in fact, slowly but surely bringing it about! Apo, does this remove the confusion for you?"

"Yes, thank you," Apo replied, adding, "So, for my clarification, it means that everything that happens is ok, spiritually-speaking. Everything leads to our spiritual expansion. Greater suffering takes longer but yields greater spiritual progress than the more even path. Are these thoughts correct?"

"Indeed, they are, Apo," Ch'askawani replied, glancing around, noticing other villagers nodding. Evidence they were understanding.

The sage-like teacher added, "Every experience has value. We either use it to overcome who we are not, or continue the false storyline which will lead to a transformation later.

"Think of the word 'attention' as 'a tension' or stress. Something to be overcome. The attention of our ancestors was on survival, to overcome starvation and early death. But once tradition established the means of survival, starvation and premature death were overcome. At that point, 'a tension', or attention, can refocus on other experiences, which can shift and expand perception of life.

"I return again and again to Miski's resurrection because it alters the idea of death. Her experience changes awareness for all those who witnessed three days of a body lying without any signs of life. No heartbeat. No breathing. Yet, the body came back to life when the Spirit re-entered it. The experience shows that, while the material side of life may die, the spiritual side endlessly exists. Her resurrection is an example of the false identification with the body. When you identify yourself as a body, you think you are dying when the body is dying. You can say from experience this idea is no longer true for you.

Ch'askawani chuckled, then added, "You could call yourself an 'IS-BE.' One always **IS** and shall always **BE**. That's not an idea, it's reality!"

7

Ru'qu and Ch'askawani were camping in the high Montane Grassland near Imanopis Llapanmama Kanqan, the sacred lake, finally alone. According to Ch'askawani's invitation, they would be camping for four or five days. It was the morning of the second day, and they sat cozily on tuffs of feathergrass a short distance away from a flock of Andean geese.

Ru'qu's thoughts drifted into the details of their amorous encounter the night before. The air had been cold, the landscape lit by a full moon. After clearing rocks near the lake for a sleeping area, Ru'qu and Ch'askawani improvised a makeshift bed by putting down feather grass thick enough to serve as a cushion; Then, they laid down a wool blanket. Another wool blanket served as the top covering.

As dark approached, they had decided to retire. Ru'qu and Ch'askawani laid side-by-side as their intimate evening began, chatting about their impressions of each other. Also, Ru'qu was curious about the earlier part of Ch'askawani's life and had questions about his knowledge of where he came from in the stars.

The longer they laid together talking, the more their amorous desires for each other grew. Finally, Ru'qu had lifted herself and leaned over, kissing Ch'askawani softly. That kiss had led to another, then another, which prompted Ru'qu to crawl on top of Ch'askawani. They had kissed again—a lengthier kiss. Ch'askawani slipped both his hands under Ru'qu's soft alpaca wool sweater, hesitantly at first, feeling the tightness of her skin and her muscles.

Ru'qu had pulled herself higher atop Ch'askawani, so her torso was over his face. Then, as an invitation, she pulled the bottom of her sweater up to her neck, exposing her firm, round breasts. Ch'askawani's hands slid off the sides of her back and found Ru'qu's breasts. Unsure, he touched them. Then, as he grasped each with his hands, Ru'qu lowered her head. Their lips melted together.

Before long, Ru'qu's skirt had come up, and Ch'askawani's pants had come down. Wrapped in each other's arms, they had quietly made love. The heat they had created in that lovemaking between those two blankets had left them sweating when they reached the end of their sexual romp.

This recall motivated her to look over at him. Feeling her eyes penetrating him, he quickly looked over at her, smiled without saying anything at first, then asked, "Anything on your mind?"

"Just thinking about you!" The tender reply as their lips met in a long kiss. Then, as they pulled apart, Ru'qu commented, "I didn't know you felt so passionate toward me until last night."

"I confess," Ch'askawani admitted, "I surprised myself. Last night happened so quickly. Before I knew what was happening, we were naked and pressed against one another. You are the first one I've had sex within this life. Yet, here I am, 50 years old. Last night was a thrill for me. I hope you enjoyed it too?"

Ru'qu tilted her head to one side shyly and blinked her eyelids a couple of times, and said, "I'd be lying if I said I didn't! You are a man from another world!"

"I never took notice of your incredible beauty until the day we met, and I felt that for the first time. After that, I wasn't sure whether I was picking up on your feelings or mine. Maybe we were feeling the same?"

"Hasn't that question been answered?" Ru'qu asked, adding, "This could be the start of a whole new life together. You are a wise man and sensitive too. I am thrilled. You would make an ideal friend and maybe life partner."

Ch'askawani stiffened his lip and thought for a moment, then nodded. "I have not thought about a mate in this life. I have ignored some urges of the body, which may be an aspect I need to explore further," he admitted, smiling.

Ru'qu leaned against him, pulling the bottom of her wool sweater out as an invitation. They kissed. His response was quick in coming. First, he slipped his hand under her knitted garment and immediately felt her firm breasts. Then, instantly aroused and getting hard, he laid against her. They immediately fell back onto the ground, and they started pulling off their clothes. So passionately involved were they for a time they didn't even notice the line of geese parading single file within a few feet of them, nor the cool breeze that began, bringing a heavy cloud cover that stole the sun's warmth. Such was their new love at that moment, oblivious to their surroundings.

After some deep passion, Ch'askawani lifted himself off Ru'qu, laughing.

With a curious face, she asked, "What?"

"My ancestors on the Chukichinchay home planet," Ch'askawani revealed, "discovered years and years ago reproductive energy is the key to longevity. The energy created by reaching climax copulating releases an enzymatic catalyst to the hormones regulating the time clock of longevity. The well-known agelessness on the home planet results from their prolific sensual activities. Why had I not thought of this fact before?"

"Well, handsome, never too late to get started," Ru'qu replied with a mischievous look. She threw her arms around his neck and pulled him back down to her.

They spent most of the remainder of the morning lying in each other's arms, partially clothed.

In the afternoon, they went for a walk, climbing the side of a nearby mountain, and when they rested, they talked more to understand one another better.

Ch'askawani began, "I came from a world in *Chukichinchay*. Here there are no marriages or family structure. Each loves and respects all without prejudice for one or another. In your world, marriage represents the reunification of the separation of masculine and feminine energies, which is gone so far as to materialize in separate forms, male and female. This physical separation is one way of experiencing the balancing of masculine and feminine energies between forms, but the greatest need is balancing those energies within oneself. Unbalance identifies the feeling of incompleteness felt by many through the desire for another in their life who will supposedly make them feel complete, as the masculine and feminine qualities are to produce a reciprocal response, a harmonious back and forth."

"I can see what you are saying," Ru'qu commented, "How different is that in the world from which you came?"

"It might sound strange to you, but on my home planet, there is no separation of bodies into male and female."

Ru'qu squinted, trying to figure out what he meant.

"Much of the evolution in the world I came from was influenced by the unique environment of a three-star system, resulting in biological androgyny in all animal life forms, which included beings like my parent, Xona. All species there are both male and female!"

"What?" Ru'qu shocked. "Seems impossible from the way my body is."

"Certainly different," Ch'askawani chuckled. "Other civilizations we have explored reportedly labeled our home a planet of bald females. All inhabitants have hemispherical breasts, which here are associated with women and have no scrotum or external testis, also associated with women here. The penis is hidden inside the vagina but protrudes upon erection. What you know as testicles, which produce sperm, and ovaries, which produce eggs, are two glands in their bodies located in the recesses of the vagina at the base of the penis. An androgynous being can insert its penis into its vagina. Sperm and ovulation activation coincide. Hence, how asexual reproduction occurs.

Ru'qu, raising her eyebrows, said, "That's unbelievable!"

"However, this orientation does not preclude two androgynous beings from having a sexual experience together, should they choose to do so. I might also add from the information we've received on my home planet, that there are androgynous humans in your planet's history who have given asexual birth, which was described as 'virgin birth' to conceal the truth."

"As strange as it sounds to me, the possibility makes sense the way you've explained it. I never thought there was any other way Quechuan women and men could have sex. But you are like us. Your sexual organs are on the outside of your body like any man here," Ru'qu said, putting her hand on his leg.

"Geneticists working on my project altered the DNA so upon my birth, I would be like any other males in your population, except for not having hair on my head."

Ru'qu playfully pulled his hat off, exposing his bald head, and shouted, "Pagla" (having no hair). Both laugh loudly about his baldness. She noticed his small ears pointed up with no lobes. *He has always worn a hat with ear flaps, probably to conserve heat.*

"I want to ask you about coming here, but before that, tell me more about masculine and feminine qualities in my world that you mentioned," Ru'qu requested.

"Are affectionate, cheerful, child-like, and compassionate descriptions of the feminine?" Ch'askawani asked.

"Yes," Ru'qu replied and further offered, "I would add flatterable... gullible ...sensitive...shy...soft-spoken...tender...and with a little more thought, sympathetic, understanding, warm, yielding, emotional, kind, and helpful."

"Agreed. However, when out of balance, these receptive qualities change into controlling, critical, manipulative, over-giving, and people-pleasing."

"Regarding masculine energy, words often used are ambitious, analytical, assertive, athletic, competitive, dominant, forceful, independent, self-reliant, self-sufficient, strong. But, on the other hand, when out of balance, they are aggressive, controlling, critical, unstable, and uncaring.

Most importantly, when a person is balanced, they display both masculine and feminine energies. A woman or a man can be receptive in one moment and assertive in another, reflecting each being as naturally flexible. The difficulty arises when out of balance. The way a person interacts with others becomes strained due to inflexibility. A sensitive person may become insensitive. A supportive person may become unsupportive. An otherwise respectful person becomes disrespectful."

"I can see what you mean, Ch'askawani," Ru'qu replied. "When I look at our tradition, it seems like there is an imbalance between men and women. Men's drunkenness and violence to women and children shout this out. Both women and children do the same work as men but are often considered servants, or are controlled. Why are men socially accepted as authority figures in family and social situations? It surprises me because women are the most creative while also doing the same labor as the men."

"You make an accurate observation, Beloved. Can people realize an ineffective quality may take on an altogether different appearance to be more effective? That a person may shift from assertive to aggressive? From being confident to being controlling? From being respectful to disrespectful? The responses to those extremes may also take on alternate expressions. When men become confrontational, women become withdrawn, less caring, less generous, less receptive, less supportive, and more critical.

"When men become demanding, women become more dependent as people-pleasers. We both see these imbalances in the village's people, which creates more imbalance until there is a breakdown in the relationship. There is social pressure to maintain relationships, which means relationships in name only, without a heartbeat. These are only hollow shells, and some appear as marriages, some friendships. When each person works on themselves, a relationship with another can thrive, not just exist."

"In talking about this, I feel a release of tension I didn't realize was in me," Ru'qu remarked. "I guess I can feel the energies of others more than I realized."

"Another clear observation you've made," Ch'askawani pointed out. "This is why what each person is thinking and feeling is important because it is energy which radiates out into the environment and is picked up by others, even imperceivable. In other words, you don't know how you feel angry, upset, sad, discontent, and so on when there is no apparent reason. It is coming from your surroundings. If you are in a group of unhappy people, what would be the energy they are giving off and you are feeling?"

"Unhappiness. Of course! It is more obvious to me now," Ru'qu said with a grateful smile.

"Yet here is an important point. You cannot repress thoughts and feelings because expressing them is the means of releasing them. They can be released forever IF you don't claim ownership of them by creating a story about them. Such as I am sad because I have a miserable life. Such a feeling is not being released but reclaims ownership of the feeling. Better to feel the sadness deeply, and it will leave naturally."

"Perfect, my love. Thank you. What an insight!" she said with a smiling face.

"Shall we walk some more?" Ch'askawani asked, interested.

"Yes, let's do it!" The eager reply.

Both jumped to their feet, embraced tightly, and kissed. Then, Ru'qu gestured for Ch'askawani to lead the way, and they rambled off.

Returning from five days of camping, which passed by all too quickly for these love birds, Ru'qu and Ch'askawani strolled joyfully down the mountain path hand in hand. The village in view, they decided to stop and relax for a while and take in the panoramic vista spread wide in front of them.

Both were bundled up in warm clothes while sitting on the camelid skins and wool blankets they'd brought. Overcast conditions had re-placed the cloudless night sky, and the cold from the previous night had not changed. With a puzzled look, Ru'qu asked, "Why were you brought to this remote place by the Ch'usaq Pacha? You could have influenced so many more in areas with large numbers of people."

"It would seem so, but which would you rather be, a big fish in a small pond or a little fish in a big pond?" Ch'askawani asked.

"I get your point, but come on, why here?"

"Explorers from Chukichinchay have been traveling to other worlds so far from here they cannot be seen in your night sky, colonizing planets in distant galaxies like *Mayu*. Unfortunately, many adven-turers are dropped off and never return to their home planet. Such a situation may happen to me as well. Only time is an excellent book of existence.

"I hope so. But maybe I want this moment to last forever. Or, the feeling of this moment," Ru'qu commented.

"I am here to create a ripple effect of my energy and my awareness to influence the evolution of all beings I meet while here. It might surprise you to hear there are many adventurers from my home planet on this planet, who over time have forgotten their home in the stars. Those of us who are 'star born' are here to 'show and tell.' Show our unique abilities and tell our special awareness as a steppingstone in the spiritual evolution of spirits lost in identifying as thoughts, feelings, desires, fears, and regrets.

"This is only the very beginning of my journey here. After this life, I will lose conscious contact with my home planet. However, through time, a memory will occur, and I will return to this same village again, as if for the first time."

"You may not fully grasp what I am about to say. The journey here and my life was pre-planned. A spiritual adventurer, not unlike you, my Beloved."

"The difference between us is so fascinating and somehow familiar," Ru'qu admits. "Maybe you're awakening me to remembering more of myself than I thought possible."

"As I said, the passage of this mysterious thing called time will tell," Ch'askawani reiterated in an optimistic tone. "Maybe someday, you will awaken me to my true self when I have lost myself in identifying as thoughts, feelings, desires, fears, and regrets! Who can say?"

Ch'askawani kissed Ru'qu once, twice, three times. Then, finally, she gave an enthusiastic nod. So up they jumped, gathered their belongings, and down the mountain slope they went, as Ru'qu yelled, "Sonqollaqta, here we come!"

While the two love birds made it home before the rains began, tears would be shed in the days ahead, making that season the wettest ever. The following few months of the rainy season would reveal dark skies, and dreary and moist environmental conditions. But this weather did little to dampen the spirit of Ru'qu. On the contrary, she remained fascinated with Ch'askawani. To her, he was as the myths portrayed Chukichinchay, a celestial god in human form. Even more reason, her heart was on fire.

The departure of Guari and Atoc to Qosqo for the rainy season was the only news that seemed unusual. They were ten-year residents of Sonqollaqta and have never taken such an extended leave. But unfortunately, they gave no word to explain their departure. Waywa reported they left a couple of days after Ru'qu and Ch'askawani departed on their camping excursion. Yet Ch'askawani saw Atoc stick his head up from behind a large boulder when he and Ru'qu were walking. He had not mentioned being spied on, not wanting to alarm her, but it had bothered him; especially with Guari and Atoc's departure news, presumably to Qosqo.

The rain fell hard for a couple of days. Finally, on the second night, Ch'askawani made his way through the rain a short distance to visit Arisi, Kuychi, and Ru'qu.

Two dark figures who stood on the corner of the compound heard Ch'askawani close the door and his outline disappeared behind a curtain of rain. They waited a while before making their way cautiously to the entrance of the 'hall.' They entered quickly and closed the door.

Meanwhile, Waywa and Manqa were at home talking about Guari's threats concerning Ch'askawani.

"I think Guari is serious about hurting Ch'askawani," Waywa said. "He said it would happen when he and Atoc were gone, and they left. I would feel terrible if something happened to him, and I didn't warn him.

"I agree. At least tell Ch'askawani what was said that day and let him judge for himself," Manqa agreed with a worried look.

"I am going over there now," Waywa jumped up, frightened.

"Wait until tomorrow. It can hold until morning. The rain is coming down hard," Manqa objected.

"No! No! I'll go!" Waywa shouted while slipping on a leather hat and leather jacket. He was out the door without another word from Manqa, hurrying through the dark and the driving rain.

Death was waiting inside the hall. One assailant stood behind the door, the other on the opposite side of the doorway. Footsteps quickly approaching were heard, splashing in the standing water. Then, finally, the door opened, and Waywa stepped in the low door-way of the room dimly by the hot coals in the central hearth. As he straightened up, he felt a sharp pain in this abdomen and an acute pain across this throat. Immediately he fell to the ground, struggling to breathe and bleeding to death as blood poured out of him.

Atoc thrusting a blade into Waywa and tearing open Waywa's guts was the last sensation felt. Before Guari slit his throat, Waywa's spirit exited the body without physical pain or emotional trauma. Instead, Waywa's spirit was floating above the scene and saw the body's final moments, twisting and squirming before appearing lifeless in a growing pool of blood. Then Waywa's spirit looked up, saw a bright light, and felt drawn toward it.

In the dim light, Guari saw Waywa's face. The raspy voice of Guari gasped, "Shit, this is Waywa, not Ch'askawani!"

"What do we do now?" Atoc begged to know.

There was no time to do anything; Ch'askawani was approaching. Then, seeing the open door and two figures standing in the hall, he asked, "What's going on here?"

Quick-witted, Guari responded, "Ch'askawani, good thing you showed up; we found Waywa bleeding and brought him here. Can you help him?"

"Yes, please stand back and let me see," Ch'askawani ordered as he bent down over the body; suddenly, he wondered why Waywa was lying face down. Instantly he realized what had happened, but it was too late. He was unexpectedly stabbed multiple times by Guari and Atoc. He had no time to yell, no time to defend himself. His blood quickly mixed with Waywa's plasma already spread on the ground.

As Ch'askawani felt the pain in his back, his spirit slipped out of his body.

Atoc released his grip on his blade in Ch'askawani's back, an eerie feeling coming over him. He looked to his right and saw Ch'askawani floating near the doorway, looking at him. Scared, Atoc yelled, "Ch'askawani is still alive!"

"Don't be crazy, man. Get a hold of yourself, Guari said, pulling the knife out of Ch'askawani's back. Then, forcefully, he sliced off a chunk of flesh from the fallen healer's hand, thrust the knife into the dirt, and slid the piece of the dying man's flesh in his pocket. "Let's get out of here," he then shouted, "We have to get as far away from this village as possible by morning. When villagers find those dead bodies, search for suspects by the enraged will begin soon after.

Out into the rain, they dashed in haste.

The subsequent events did not take as long to unfold as Guari predicted.

Where is Waywa? Manqa had fallen asleep and, after waking up, suddenly wondered. Glancing around, Manqa didn't see Waywa. He panicked, thinking, *He should be back by now*. But to find out for sure, he'd have to go to Ch'askawani's compound where Waywa purportedly headed when they last talked. Unsettled, Manqa decided to do just that. He slipped on a poncho and hat. As he opened the door, he was pleased to notice the rain had stopped. He ran as fast as he could. As he got to the open doorway, grief stopped him, and he fell to his knees, weeping profusely. He knew the unimaginable had taken place. He knew even without identifying the two bodies, he knew.

Manqa stood up and stepped in when tears reduced to sobbing.

To fully see the tragedy before him, he immediately took wood off the woodpile in the corner of the hall and threw chunks on the hot ashes to get a fire going to increase the light in the room. He saw Ch'askawani's body lying diagonally on top of Waywa's. The back of Ch'askawani's wool shirt was blood-soaked. He felt his neck for a pulse. He felt none. Ch'askawani was dead, he was sure.

Weeping again, Manqa seeing Waywa's body face down was almost unbearable. He could see the killer had cut Waywa's throat, and in a pool of his blood, he lay. Manqa froze. He cried more tears than he thought possible and could do nothing else for a long time except sob, but, finally, his tears subsided. For the first time in his life, he felt useless. What was there to do now? Nothing! Nothing mattered. The two most important people he knew lay dead. He wanted to kill himself.

Manqa, standing outside Arisi's door, reluctantly waited, mustering enough courage to tell Arisi such regrettably lousy news. Manqa was feeling his life had already been destroyed, telling Arisi, Kuychi, and Ru'qu would ruin theirs too. But he knew hesitating longer would not change things. How could he stop the unbearable grief so many others were about to experience? He couldn't. Manqa began pounding on the door.

The noise woke Arisi. He was reluctant to get out of bed, still sleepy. But curiosity pulled him up and out of bed. Finally, he got to the door and opened it.

"Arisi, it's me, Manqa," the dark figure said.

"Manqa, what's so urgent you have to get me out of bed at this hour?

"Ch'askawani and Waywa are dead!" he blurted out.

Arisi gasped. He couldn't believe it and said, "I saw him earlier in the evening. What possibly could have happened?"

"Someone murdered them," Manqa added.

Stunned and confused, Arisi wanted to spare his wife and daughter the shocking news without details. He turned to see if they were behind him or if they might have heard what was said. Almost whispering, he replied nervously, "I need to see for myself. I'll put on clothes and be right out."

"Arisi, what's going on?" Kuychi asked, wakened by the disturbance, and sitting on the edge of the bed next to Ru'qu.

Wanting to appear calm to his wife and daughter but unsure of what to say, his response was vague, "I'm not sure, but it doesn't look good."

His answer led Kuychi to ask further, "Arisi, are you alright?".

Afraid he would 'let the cat out of the bag,' he said nothing more. Arisi was out of the house, closing the door behind him, and disappeared into the night with Manqa.

Kuychi looked at Ru'qu sitting alongside her on the edge of the bed, "Honey, something is wrong when Arisi is unwilling to tell me what is going on. Let's get dressed and find out for ourselves what the secrecy is all about?"

"But mama, we don't know where they went," Ru'qu reflected.

"I think I know," Kuychi replied as she lifted herself off the bed to dress.

Deeply shaken by the news, Arisi hurried with Manqa the short distance to the compound. But the closer they got, the slower Arisi's movement, dreading what he would see. But he thought to himself, *to avoid accepting what has already happened is impossible.* He took a deep breath. In two strides, they were at the doorway. Manqa went in first. Putting a hand on each side of the door frame to hold himself up, Arisi hung his head in abject sorrow at what he saw. Tears streamed down his cheeks as he wept bitterly. Manqa stood motionless like a statue on the other side of the two bodies, his eyes glazed while watching his friend. He knew Arisi's distress. It was his own.

"Who could have done such a thing?" Manqa asked in an even, emotionless tone.

But Arisi wasn't listening. The blade still sticking in Ch'askawani's back and the other one stuck in the ground next to his arm caught Arisi's attention.

Immediately recognizing both blades, he said, "I think I have just realized who the killers are," as he knelt close to the dead. Then he continued, "A month earlier in Paucartambo, I traded for two sharp pieces of metal, wanting them as souvenirs. But, upon returning home and mentioning them in passing to Guari, he asked to purchase them from me as gifts, he said, for relatives in Qosqo. So, I recognize these two pieces of metal. They belong to Guari!"

"From what I've heard, what you said makes sense," Manqa responded.

"What have you heard?" A curious look on Arisi's face.

"The day following Ch'askawani healing my broken shoulder, I went for a walk on the mountainside after talking to him. Waywa had also taken a walk up the slope without me knowing it.

"I saw Waywa sitting on the slope below me when I was near the village," Manqa explained, "Guari was standing over him, making aggressive gestures. When I got within hearing range, I heard Guari threatening him. After making myself known to them, I challenged Guari's threat. He changed his tune, said he was only kidding, but his main point to Waywa was his prediction of Ch'askawani's demise. After Guari left us, Waywa explained that Guari and Atoc had a plan to get rid of Ch'askawani. The beauty of the scheme, Guari said, smiling, was not being around when it happened, so there would be no accusation of involvement with the death."

"Huh," Arisi was thinking, then said, "Maybe saying they were going to be gone was just a smokescreen he concocted to throw suspicion in any direction but theirs."

Manqa's words added more direct evidence to Arisi's suspicion that Guari and Atoc were the assailants, infuriating him.

At that moment, Arisi looked at Ch'askawani's hand close to the blade stuck in the ground. Then, he hollered, "That *supay* (creature of hell)! He cut off the one finger identifying Ch'askawani as a god!" Outraged, Arisi pounded the ground several times with his fist.

Hearing deafening screams that began from behind him, he stopped. He stood and whirled around, knowing Kuychi and Ru'qu had arrived. Dashing past him, Ru'qu fell on Ch'askawani's lifeless form. He was able to grab Kuychi and pull her tightly to him as she screamed. Both were beyond consoling with words. *Crying seems the way to relieve grief*, Arisi thought, *there is no sparing them their sorrow. I can barely deal with my own.*

From that crushing moment, misery spread rapidly through the village like floodwaters. Many were confused with unanswered questions; others were terrified someone in their small settlement was capable of such a wicked and hateful act. Still, those closest to the deceased were devastated, emotionally torn to shreds. Healing seemed a long way away for any. Yet certain painful things needed accomplishing, such as cleaning the bodies and preparing a funeral. Sadly, most of this burden was in the hands of those most overwhelmed.

The savage brutality of the killings was evident when Arisi, Kuychi, Ru'qu, and Manqa removed the clothing of the dead. Stabbed in the stomach and his throat slit, Waywa must have been mistaken for Ch'askawani, the actual intended victim. Ch'askawani, leaning over Waywa when assailed, was stabbed multiple times, and had the extra finger on his left hand sliced off. The savage act of removing a body part was the killer's final attempt to humiliate, as if he were an enemy of the killer.

"There is one more thing to do before the funeral," Arisi explained to Kuychi, Ru'qu, and Manqa. "Ch'askawani requested should he die before me that his body was to be cremated, not buried. So, I will need to construct a funeral pyre and lay his body on it for viewing. Manqa, did Waywa have a request regarding disposal?"

"No, but aware that body and spirit are separate, it seems to me to burn the body is a purifying ending. He can't return to ashes!" Manqa.

"That makes sense to me, Manqa," Kuychi offered.

"And I agree," Ru'qu added.

"Me too," Arisi agreed, adding, "So it will be: Two funeral pyres will be built! I will round up all the help I need to construct the pyres, and the funeral should be ready within two days."

As anticipated, the two pyres stood ready on time. In addition, several runners went out announcing the funeral. Orchids traded for in the lowlands came. Several Sonqollaqta women offered colorful blankets on which the bodies of the two deceased would lay.

"Friends, this is an occasion that resulted from a shockingly terrible circumstance. The double-murder of two men who are neighbors and friends of most of us and life-long residents of the settlement. These were tragedies."

These words were the beginning of Arisi's eulogy.

"Waywa, who had been an unhappy drunkard for years, was beginning a new life of sobriety. Ch'askawani was both a messenger and a message for an expanding quality of life, most of us unaware it existed until he enlightened us. But unfortunately, neither he nor his miraculous work was close to being completed.

"I feel incapable of singing the praises of a god from the stars who brought a message to life with his actions. Living with an Apu-Runa (a Godman) is the closest we get to the heavenly realm while in this body. We are forever grateful to the Ch'usaq Pacha for choosing our village as the place to bestow the celestial gift of Ch'askawani. When Kuychi accepted him into her arms and the rest of us into our lives, a remarkable journey began with a baby boy from the Ch'usaq Pacha fifty years ago.

As Arisi spoke, he scanned the crowd and saw disappointment, despair, sorrow, sadness, and regret written on the faces in the group. He also heard weeping, sniffling, and sobbing, for which he hesitated, acknowledging those visibly suffering.

"The overcast sky is most appropriate for this day of mourning. Indeed, this is the rainy season, but today more water will fall from our eyes than the skies.

"For those who might have wondered what horror did Waywa and Ch'askawani experience in their final moments, Ch'askawani once told me, in a painful situation, whether physical or emotional, the spirit moves partially or totally out of the body. So, considering what their bodies may have endured is no indication of what they had undergone.

"One other thing, Waywa and Ch'askawani would have observed and identified the killers. Not only did Manqa hear Guari say he had a plan for disposing of Ch'askawani after murdering him, but the spirit of Ch'askawani also appeared to me in a dream and told me Atoc and Guari were the culprits. So, if anyone sees them, they should notify the village elders immediately.

"We also know from Manqa, Waywa went to the compound that night to warn Ch'askawani of the possibility of impending danger. The two killers must have already been there, waiting for Ch'askawani, who visited my family and me for a short time that evening. Waywa, on his errand of mercy, was mistaken for Ch'askawani and killed shortly before Ch'askawani's return and his subsequent murder.

"Raising the dead, restoring sight to the blind, healing broken bones were a few of the remarkable healings. Hundreds benefited from Ch'askawani's healing powers over the years. In addition, his words of wisdom spared many continued lives under old worn-out perspectives that resulted in monotony and boredom, and the subsequent drinking and domestic violence that plagued the village. I express gratitude for all that Ch'askawani did.

"We are better for having had him in our lives and losing him, than not having him at all. I suspect this was the intent of the Ch'usaq Pacha to expand our awareness. So may his purpose be known widely in his future lifetimes, and may we live our lives more as he proposed. Love is more than words; it is deeds. So, for those who respected him, may our consolation perpetuate his teaching and reproduce his actions.

"Enough said. Light the fires and may only good arise from the ashes," Arisi concluded.

Many villagers suffered the days and weeks following the murders, which hit Ru'qu the hardest, shattering a fantasy life with Ch'askawani. Instead, moments of spontaneous and uncontrollable anxiety and tears replaced that dream. Her parents suspected heartbreak, but what could they do? While struggling to cope with their pain, their daughter's mental and emotional health concerned them.

They hoped her reaction to the death of Ch'askawani wasn't shaping the direction her life would take, trusting she would not keep returning to her impressions of that terrifying night's loss. However, they knew, as it was for them, Ch'askawani's untimely death would be the most painful memory she'd carry the rest of her life.

Weeks later, Ru'qu awoke in the middle of the night, yelling for her parents. "Poppy, mama," she shouted gleefully.

Alarmed at first, both parents sat up in bed, eagerly attentive to their daughter.

"What is it, child?" Kuychi asked.

"What, my love?" Arisi begged.

Anguish had not awakened her as the parents thought, but joy.

"I had the most wonderful dream. Ch'askawani appeared in his glorious form, indicating we would be together again soon, which filled me with peace and hope but puzzled me also. How could such a reunion possibly happen?"

His puzzling words stymied all three.

The eyes of both Kuychi and Arisi narrowed as they tried without success to guess the meaning. Ru'qu was just overjoyed, feeling the dream confirmed her statement made to Ch'askawani the day they talked on the way to the last village gathering, when she had said, maybe we'll be together in the future.

Two days later, the houses of both Atoc and Guari and the compound burned down, which surprised everyone. No one took responsibility for the acts, and no one knew who the arsonist might have seen. Arisi wondered if it was the unseen hand of the spirit of Ch'askawani—A thought he kept to himself.

A week later, the village elders unanimously agreed to confiscate Atoc's and Guari's properties and turn them into community property. Crops on these properties would be grown by the shared responsibility of the community members and the proceeds used for community functions.

As time passed, the whole village appeared to heal. Some moved away, and others moved on with their lives. But the one thing that did the most to heal Arisi, Kuychi, and Ru'qu was when Ru'qu announced to her mother that she was probably pregnant. She had no menstruation for the second month in a row.

Arisi's immediate response was, "I think we may have the answer to what Ch'askawani meant in your dream!"

8

Ch'askancha mumbled half-crying as he awoke from a frightening dream. His eyes were tearful, and his nose was dripping mucus. The 10-year-old boy was frightened and trembling.

As he lay in bed, his body quivering, he thought to himself, *A faceless figure with a deep voice asking me, where is your tayta (father)? It's one in many faces I have seen in many dreams asking me the same question. A collection of faces unlike any I've ever seen before pulled off what appeared as their masks to see all revealing my face, each face asking, where is your tayta? Where is your tayta? Where is your tayta? Such dreams scare me,* he thought, *I DON'T EVEN HAVE A TAYTA! So, what do these recurring dreams mean? Is it something good or bad?*

Ch'askancha desperately wanted to wake up his mother, Ru'qu, and tell her, but couldn't. All the other times the dreams occurred, they prompted the thought that she may be the reason why these dreams keep happening.

Over three years ago, he thought, *I asked mama, why don't I have a tayta? Her response was she'd tell me when I was old enough to understand. I don't want to blame her, but these dreams started after that. I wish these dreams to stop and this dark figure and his question to go away. That goes for these weird faces and their questions, too.*

Ch'askancha sniffled, wiped his eyes with the back of his hand, and began to feel a little relief. Then he shivered. The cold, almost a nightly condition, finally got his attention, infiltrating the heavy wool blanket covering the bed, and he felt that early morning hour. "Sleep is over for me," Ch'askancha said. He threw the blanket off, sitting on the edge of the bed in a pensive mood. "Burrrrrrrr," he said. Then, quickly jumping up, he grabbed his knee-length wool pants, slid into them, and pulled on a heavy wool sweater.

Looking in the direction of the hearth, Ch'askancha noticed a few red embers glowing in the otherwise dark interior of the one-room house. Starting the fire would be much easier and faster than from scratch. The boy smiled, stood up, and walked barefooted across the cold dirt floor, not bothered because thick calluses had developed on his feet.

He quickly gathered an armful of twigs from a pile of kindling next to the door and placed those twigs over the embers and blew gently. Flames erupted. Ch'askancha rubbed my hands together over the burgeoning fire to warm them, and then he added more twigs along with a larger piece of wood.

Glancing over at the bed, barely seen in the faint firelight, there was no movement. Ch'askancha's mama was still asleep. He was surprised, thinking, *mama instinctively wakes up just before dawn, the habit of most of the inhabitants of the village.*

As dawn approached, everyone stood outside their houses leaning against their east walls awaiting the earliest rays of the morning sun to warm them once it shone over the eastern horizon.

Walking to the door and opening it, he stuck his head out. The black curtain of the night still hung over the landscape, and stars were still visible in the night sky. "Earlier than I thought," the boy commented under his breath. What was he to do?

Wide awake and disturbed by his dream, the boy wanted more time to contemplate the entire matter of not having a tayta. Instantly, he got the idea of taking the family's small herd of alpacas farther into the mountains on one of several paths, the one leading to the sacred lake—the boy's favorite place. He thought, *allowing them to graze is so much easier than cutting feathergrass and bringing it to them. Besides, we'll be back by dark easily. Moreover, the montane grassland is good pasture for the alpacas, and* an *excellent day to freely think.* So, Ch'askancha put on the needed clothing.

As Ch'askancha came to know it, the traditional attire was an adaptation insulating him from the harsh condition of a high altitude—the cold. Aside from the wool pants and heavy wool sweater, he added the Quechuan-style wool hat with earflaps—his longish black hair sticking out along the edges of the cap. Over the wool sweater, he slipped on a wool poncho covering the upper portion of his body.

After tying a blue string to the door latch, a "note" to his mother, indicating he had gone off with the alpacas to mountain pastureland, the door was closed, and Ch'askancha proceeded to the stone-walled corral.

This lad was tall for the age of 10, standing over a "head" length taller than the other boys his age, who were short and stocky. Ch'askancha's body had a sturdy build with broad shoulders and plenty of muscle developed from the strenuous physical work required of the Quechuan agrarian lifestyle he'd had started at a much younger age. Boys become 'men' early in Quechuan culture.

Approaching the corral gate at dark twilight, Ch'askancha could barely make out the outlines of the alpacas, all kneeling, exposing nothing but their thick wool coats to the freezing night air, their legs tucked under their bodies. The noise of the gate abruptly opening awakened the alpacas. They turned their heads in that direction and instinctively got up. Each stretched and defecated, issuing the odor of warm gas from fresh manure which did not bypass the boy's approach as it traveled through the air. Ch'askancha wrinkled his nose.

Ch'askancha and his herd appeared as dark figures in the gray twilight, silently moving westward along the mountainside above Sonqollaqta to reach the higher montane grassland used for grazing camelids.

Slowly, the gray twilight gave way to growing light.

Watching the alpacas' movements, the young Quechuan fixated on their normal jerky motion as they moved to snatch bites of feathergrass found scattered here and there in the rocky terrain. He hurried them along, thinking, there's *much more feathergrass ahead in the montane grassland*.

Yet Ch'askancha decided to pause and look back at the entire village in the distance, stretched out across his field of vision, only part of a larger scene of nature—A thrill for him every time.

One, two, three, four..., Ch'askancha counted to himself, *...Thirty-five houses*. "That's the whole village," he said as if talking to the alpacas, "Aren't they beautiful, tucked in among the cultivated fields, the corrals, and patches of shrubs and trees?" He liked to count the number of houses. He did each time he took the trail, impressed as he was by the view.

Rays from the rising sun poured over the landscape, casting an otherworldly light over his homeland. "What a sight!" He exclaimed. "The houses and the lower hills to the east are all bathed with the sun's golden light." This scene never ceased to captivate, and he said so out loud, "I am a part of this beauty. Every time I see this view, I am thankful to the spirits and gods of this world for allowing me to be part of it."

After some silence, the boy questioned himself, *why am I bothered by a reoccurring dream when this*, spreading his arms to take in all that was before him, *is my life?* Ch'askancha shrugged his shoulders. He didn't have an answer. He felt a cold breeze on his face, followed by heat from the warming sun. He chuckled, "My life is these differences."

He turned around to proceed onward. Immediately he noticed all the alpacas had stopped foraging and were staring at him. "Maybe they understand more about me than I understand about them. Sometimes they act like companions!" were his concluding words spoken softly as he and the herd began moving upward again.

The young boy was feeling the pride of his heritage. Quechuans were farmers and herdsmen. Cultivating the land and raising livestock provided all the necessities of life: food, clothing, and shelter. Moreover, his homeland in the Andes Mountains was biologically diverse. As a result, minor variations in the adaptation contributed to its overall success, explaining why the tradition has remained unchanged for thousands of years. Over time, the resourcefulness of the Quechuans was their ability to comprehend what they had to contend with and adjust to conditions in the most ingenious ways.

While Ch'askancha expected the cold start to the day, he noticed the cloudless blue sky that made the snow-capped mountain peaks in the distant west glisten. A gust of chilling wind out of the East was at his back. Feeling a slight chill on his neck, he gave thanks for his warm clothes. "To the spirits that watch over me, my family, and my land, thank you for all that keeps us warm."

He was musing about the alpacas. They were of great importance to his way of life. Domesticated 4,200 years before Ch'askancha's time, these camelids were used as a source of meat and sheared for their durable and thick wool hair fibers used to make knitted and woven products like shawls, sweaters, pants, hats, gloves, and more. In addition, they were very well adapted to high altitude conditions, feeding on herbs, shrubs, grasses, and lichens that grow here.

The morning air, a churning mixture of gusts of cold air from high altitude, and currents of air warmed by the sun made the alpacas and the boy spontaneously frisky. He bolted up the path, and the alpacas responded in like manner. Then, as he ran, a burst of energy made him laugh. He glanced around at the alpacas, who were bucking and jumping at irregular intervals as they galloped past him.

Exhaling loudly, he came to a sudden stop. Smiling broadly, he watched the alpacas as they continued romping ahead of him before slowing to a trot, then stopping. All the camelids craned their necks in his direction as if waiting to see what Ch'askancha would do next.

By mid-morning, the group was not very far from Imanopis Ilapan kamakanqan, the sacred lake.

The day was considerably warmer. The herd's movement had slowed to a crawl as they had reached an altitude where the montane grassland began, where feathergrass, used as fodder for the alpacas and as thatch for roof covering, was endemic and abundant, so there was stationary grazing rather than foraging. In response to the camelid's actions, Ch'askancha lazily moved, watching a Condor floating on air currents high above.

Suddenly, Ch'askancha heard that troubling echo in his mind: "Where's your tayta? Where's your tayta? Where's your tayta?" Never had an aspect of his dreams intruded upon his daytime. But this echo was only a prelude to what came next.

The young boy bent over and gathered a handful of small stones to throw. He began slowly throwing them, one after the other. Then, unexpectedly, a memory in motion started playing in his mind—a scene of three years earlier.

He had finished cultivating one of the family's potato fields and was walking down the edge of the field to the path leading back into the village. Done cultivating for the day and ready to go home, four or five boys had gathered, standing on the trail, talking amongst themselves. Ch'askancha approached and greeted them. What happened next was not expected. The boys immediately began taunting him.

The littlest boy started, "My tayta showed me how to shear llamas."

Immediately followed by another, "My tayta carries the heavy bundles of potatoes I can't even lift."

Then another, "My tayta took me hunting for deer in the high mountains."

"My tayta, my tayta, my tayta......," Ch'askancha repeated those words angrily, self-conscious about not having a father. Then he asked them, "So, what's your point?" as he looked at each of them.

Then the fourth boy responded sarcastically, "You must have a tayta. How could you be here if you didn't have a tayta?"

All the boys gave a half-suppressed, scornful laugh.

Throwing a rock to the ground as hard as he could, Ch'askancha yelled, "Enough!" He was enraged and ready to explode, the memory of that day drawing out a deep rage.

The volume and tone of his voice disrupted the grazing of the alpacas. They abruptly looked in his direction as an instinctive response to danger and stared for a while. Finally, the alpacas returned to grazing when no other sound or movement from the boy was forthcoming.

Ch'askancha kicked the dirt, upset by the memory as he was three years earlier, but at this moment, even more. Three years of these haunting dreams had him on edge. He was furious. Feeling his anger deeply, he just stood quietly, feeling it. Ch'askancha took a deep breath and exhaled. Then his mind began the memory again, reviewing the details from when he arrived home later that afternoon.

I told her about what happened with the boys and how angry I was. I had shouted at her, "Mama, why don't I have a tayta?"

Ch'askancha's memory was vivid, recalling his mama's decision to postpone answering his question. *Son, I'll tell you the whole story when you are old enough to understand what I must say to you. Please trust me on this. The time has not yet come to reveal not only your past, but your future! Therefore, I cannot give you a short answer. Once a piece of the story is explained to you, you'll beg to know the whole story.*

The boy even recalled his grandpa Arisi's words about his mother. *You've respected and accepted her words as guidance because you've witnessed her wisdom and compassion regularly.*

His grandpa's words were correct. He knew it. *I'm just having a hard time accepting the unpleasant and upsetting dreams that have been occurring since they may have value in understanding my situation of being without a tayta.*

With all these thoughts and emotions rolling around, tumbling, and mixing, in Ch'askawani's mind, he suddenly yielded to needed insight. *Wait a minute, have I missed something? I'm upset with my mama for not telling me the whole story. I don't understand ugly beings in my dreams or what those boys are getting at in saying, 'You had to have a tayta!' I must be blind! Not having a tayta doesn't deny that at some point, I had one. Besides, my mama was only protecting me. Wow, so simple. I just could not understand before. These thoughts make things more straightforward for me.*

Now maybe I can, more relaxed, talk to mama. Three years have passed. I have more insight. Hopefully, mama is ready to tell me the whole story, and I am prepared to accept the unknown.

A sudden calm came over him, the needed shift in mood.

Standing amid the montane feather grass, Ch'askancha was finally coming to grips with a life issue that had been haunting him in his dream time for three years. Part of that resolution was him feeling old enough to know the whole story. He felt fully confident for the first time in quite a while.

He thought, *today* is *the perfect day to talk to mama about not having a tayta. Indeed, she'll understand. Asked to do a man's work, I am old enough to talk about this unusual situation.*

So much of the emotional turmoil was resolved for Ch'askancha while out in nature. He smiled, relieved.

The alpacas were grazing a short distance away from the mountain pass to cross over to the beautiful mountain lake--Imananopis Llapan Kamakanqan (Miracle of Creation). According to Quechuan folklore and others in the village, the lake was sacred because **the Ch'usaq Pacha (Celestial Gods) had contacted the villagers there**. The thought excited him. He quickened his pace to catch up.

The herd and their shepherd crossed over the saddle, bringing the lake in full view.

Ch'askancha smiled broadly at the unique beauty of the shore-line. Biodiversity, unlike the surrounding area of barren rock, inter-spersed with lumps of feathergrass.

The dense grasses growing at the lake's edge were not the dry straw texture and appearance of the feather grass found on most of the grassland. Instead, the grasses on the lake's shore formed a green, lush ring around the deep blue water of the lake.

Not far from the water's edge, green tussock grasses grow in clumps, cushions, and low stalkless rosettes. Many other plants, covered with hairs shielding growing tissue from the intense solar radiation, trapped any moisture in the air. An abundance of silvery-colored rosettes was an adaptation, reflecting rather than absorbing the harsh sunlight. Some of the diverse plants had leathery leaves, and waxy coatings are also a means of preventing water loss in that semi-arid, high-altitude environment.

Ch'askancha's blue eyes scanned the terrain. The bright green and colorful vegetation thinned out quickly, moving from the lake's shoreline in concentric circles. Rocks looked cemented together with lichens and mosses as a transition before giving way to bare rock and feather grass, otherwise predominant.

As the young Quechuan had learned very early in life, and as all other mountain dwellers who live at high altitudes have learned, all the variations of flora are adaptive patterns developed to ad-just to a common climatic condition: cold. In his memory, he could hear his grandpa Arisi saying, *While the day length varies little at high elevation, the change from day to night temperature could be and is often dramatic and drastic. As much as sixty degrees could separate the daytime high from the nighttime low. While there is no prolonged period of cold to induce plant dormancy, "winter" often occurs at night!*

On reaching the lake, Ch'askancha sat on a large boulder not far from the water's edge, giving a vantage point from where he could see the entire herd. The alpacas were either standing in the water drinking or eating the lush young vegetation growing on the lake's edge.

Then movement on the shoreline to his left caught his attention. A small flock of Andean geese standing away from the shore. The duck-like geese, primarily terrestrial and avoided swimming, were inhabitants living near the lake in small communities. They had nested on the bare rocks near the shore. The boy saw them every time he came to the lake. These birds had small pink bills, white plumage, except black on their wings and tails, with heavily built bodies.

Ch'askancha remembered how surprised he was when telling his grandpa of the first time he spotted the Andean geese. Arisi had told him the geese live in the high-altitude montane grassland because they were a grazing species, eating feathergrass!

Shifting his gaze, taking in a broader view of the lake, the young boy recalled that his grandpa, Arisi, one of the elders of the village, had given the most respected name to this lake in honor of a visitation by Ch'usaq Pacha from the stars the very night of their visit.

Grandpa *Arisi* was a young lad in his mid-twenties at the time and was more directly involved in communicating with the celestial gods than his modesty permitted him to say to his grandson.

The boy recalled his grandpa saying, "Ch'usaq Pacha ('Gods' from the stars) landed somewhere near the lake's edge only sixty years earlier."

Ch'askancha was jealous. He wondered, *why was I not born to experience that?* The question caused a surge of excitement to race through his body.

These thoughts and feelings revitalized the boy every time he came to the sacred spot, and he made the sojourn at least once every five or six days.

I'm in harmony with the energy here, Ch'askancha said to himself, energetically tied to the place without understanding why.

He was confused and puzzled too. *Those who experienced these "gods" for themselves are not as excited as I imagined they would be*, Ch'askancha remembered saying to Ru'qu, *the excitement of those present at the landing that eventful night seems dampened when I ask them to talk about it. Her response, only a silent nod.*

As if mentally trying to connect the dots, the young Quechuan immediately recalled a cluster of buildings a short distance from his house. The buildings had been abandoned before he was born for reasons left unexplained. They were ruins. Free-standing adobe walls. No roof supports or thatching. Grass grew inside and on top of the partly fallen adobe walls. There were twelve buildings in total.

Ch'askancha recollected the day his curiosity pulled him to investigate the ruins, like metal to a magnet. *Even though mama had cautioned me to stay away, curiosity had gotten the best of me. On that day, I noticed the remaining parts of the roof structures were charred pieces of wood laying inside the remains of each building. All the facilities had the same appearance, without exception. So, fire must have swept through the buildings, destroying them. But why weren't they rebuilt? Why was a massive blaze that would have been caused, not part of local Quechua folklore? The only thing mama said was the members of Sonqollaqta had gone through changes just before my birth with some folks leaving who never returned. She withheld more of the details.*

Suddenly the question occurred to him, which he expressed aloud, "Was this event in any way tied to the matter of him not having a father? Hummmm."

Colder afternoon weather made itself known as a cold gust of wind. Chilled, Ch'askancha gathered the herd to begin heading back to the village.

The herder and his herd of alpacas moved steadily descending to the village on the return trip.

Approaching the village, Ch'askancha came upon the cultivated fields following the descent of the slope on both sides of the trail.

The boy saw familiar faces cultivating in the fields as he passed. Those working in the patches would look up and wave a friendly hello. The boy returned their gestures.

*S*topping for a moment and looking back at those bent over in the field above him cultivating potatoes, the youngster thought to himself, *there's a picture of life's story. Young and old working side-by-side, helping each other through life. But it also shows a person works from a young age through old age.*

Even as a boy, Ch'askancha already possessed a profound understanding, firmly aware that his life in this tradition was a thankless effort. Surviving was all the thanks he would get.

He looked down at the ground, continuing his train of thought; *this life is a repetition of what started at about age 4 or 5—the old teaching the young who, in turn, teach it to their young for the survival of the tradition to continue unbroken. The Quechuan tradition* required participation and demanded effort and endurance from children and adults. He counted them off, and he knew them very well:

raising alpacas,

cultivating fields,

planting crops and harvesting crops,

assisting relatives in their labors,

repairing houses and corrals and building new structures,

working on community-held lands,

weaving cloth on a loom,

preparing meals,

gathering firewood and water,

shearing alpacas for wool.

The work is endless.

Shrugging his shoulders as a sign of hopelessness, he turned toward the homeward direction and walked on. The alpacas had continued ahead of him and arranged themselves into a single file. They remained that way until entering the stone corral, still some distance away.

Ch'askancha's mother, Ru'qu, stood in front of their house watching her son's approach with the herd. She had come outside to grab an armful of firewood for the hearth to begin preparation of the evening meal when she noticed them coming. She waited to embrace her son.

Standing next to the woodpile, mother and son warmly greeted each other with a smile and a hug, happy to see the other. Finally, the boy released his mother and said, "Mama, I am hungry.".

"Me too," she replied. Then bent down and gathered an arm full of wood before returning to the house.

Once the entire herd was in the corral, a rectangular 6-foot-high stone wall structure that provided safety from potential predators, Ch'askancha closed the gate of sturdy wood branches tied together with rope and secured it. Then, as if by habit, he looked to his left in the direction of his grandpa Arisi's house, a short distance from the family corral. The boy knew his grandfather was away on a trip down the mountain slope, so he did not expect to see him. He walked over to the woodpile from the corral gate to gather more wood to carry in the house. With an armful, he stood up and walked toward the house.

Entering the open doorway was awkward. The door openings were shorter than he was. Short doors were an adaptation to the cold, to prevent heat from escaping. The house was without a chimney, so the door was the only means for the smoke from the central hearth to exit. So, to negotiate the doorway, the boy had to bend his head and upper body downward and step up over a six-inch sill simultaneously. The top of the door opening was about four feet high off the ground.

Dropping the wood on a pile near the door, Ch'askancha turned toward his mother, stoking the fire. The family used the fire's heat in food preparation. The fire was also the only source of light and of heat, enabling dwellers to eat, work, relax, and rest comfortably.

Ch'askancha watched the smoke from the flames rise into the rafters and reach the peak of the ceiling, which was the underside of the thatched roof, and then curled downward. The heavy smoke filled the upper portion of the house, coming down as far as the upper edge of the door opening where it exited the house. The line of carbon that marked the upper portion of the house was the same height as the top of the door. As Ch'askancha knew, once the upper part of the house was filled with smoke and began exiting underneath the top of the door frame, he would have to walk stooped, or kneel, or sit to avoid breathing in the accumulating fumes.

Ch'askancha passed the central hearth and proceeded to the far side of the room to gather the papas (potatoes) and other tubers needed. He dug his hands into several large twig-woven baskets lined up along that wall containing papas or other tubers, including olluco, oca, and mashwa. Dried leaves from these plants were for salads and making soup.

The boy's eyes darted rather excitedly from one basket to another, his hunger growing as he decided how many of each kind to choose. Then, finally, he salivated, thinking about eating the evening meal.

The youngster reached into the basket of *papas* he wanted to draw from, pulling out twenty or so in a make-shift pouch formed by lifting the lower edge of his heavy wool shirt, creating an empty container he quickly filled. Then he reached into the basket of *oca*, grabbing a couple of handfuls.

Having made his selections, Ch'askancha turned around and carried them to Ru'qu. Then, kneeling on both knees, he emptied the *papas* and the *ocas* onto the dirt floor beside his mama, who was preparing water in two separate ceramic pots, both pots setting on the hot ashes for boiling *papas* and making soup. As Ru'qu dropped the papas and the ocas in individual pots, Ch'askancha returned to the baskets for *mashwa*.

After gathering a fistful *of mashwa*, he grabbed some oca, then dipped into another basket for a bundle of dried *mashwa* leaves.

Ch'askancha returned to his mother's side with the additional items. Not seeing any *chuno*, Ru'qu looked at her son, "How about some *chuno* to put in the stew?" Ru'qu knew she and her son enjoyed the freeze-dried papa, chuno, for its slightly fermented taste, which added variety to the meal's flavor.

"Yes, mama," the boy answered in an excited tone and quickly fetched the *chuno*.

Besides the large assortment of domesticated *papas* cultivated and eaten in the Andean Highlands at that time, many Quechuans in the Andes, like the inhabitants of *Sonqo*llaqta, ate wild *papas* as added nourishment. Ch'askancha's family was no different in this regard.

With the meal preparation ending, Ru'qu poured the water off the boiled papas just outside the open door, and Ch'askancha served up bowls of thick vegetable soup for his mother and himself. Ru'qu spread the papas on a piece of leather laid on the dirt floor in front of a 6-foot-long wood log set back from the hearth about three feet that served as seating. At the same time, her son placed a bowl of stew on each side of the sprawled papas. They were left untouched until they cooled down, and Ch'askancha grabbed two wool skins from the bed and draped them over the log where he and his mother were about to eat. An aroma rose from the food that enticed Ch'askancha and Ru'qu. However, hunger was the only invitation they needed.

As they quietly began to eat, Ch'askancha's concerns earlier in the day resurfaced. He felt it was an excellent time to open discussion with his mother, a moment he awaited. Just then, attention shifted to noise heard outside the open door.

The animals had suddenly become restless and noisy. Then mother and son heard an unexpected yet familiar voice saying, "Hello."

Stooped forward in the open doorway stood *Asiri*, announcing himself before entering. Unexpectedly, he had just returned from a trip down the slope.

"Awki (grandfather)!" Ch'askancha excitedly shouted, not expecting him for another day or two.

"Are you just returning, tayta?" Ru'qu asked.

"Yes," Arisi replied with a broad smile, adding, "Instead of one more night sleeping with the llamas on the trail, I decided to finish the walk home even though it meant walking the last portion of the trail in the dark."

"We are glad you decided to come home tonight," his daughter answered joyously.

An enterprising individual, *Arisi* was one of those who spent part of his life trading goods as an aside. He was short and stocky, only an eyebrow taller than his grandson. His attire was traditional: A hat with earflaps, dark wool pants, a multi-colored wool sweater, and a colorful poncho.

He used *chuno* and alpaca wool as barter as a trader for rare goods available at a lower elevation on the eastern slope. Unusual items, either difficult to make or impossible to procure, include feathers, bone utensils, ceramic ware, metal objects, feathers, precious stones, and more.

He'd departed days earlier with two llamas, each packing three sacks, one of chuno, and two of wool and walked down the mountainside a goodly distance (17 miles while dropping 4 ,000 feet in elevation) to the larger settlement of *Paucartambo* on the banks of the *Rio Paucartambo.*

Arisi's unexpected arrival, while pleasing the boy, brought out ambivalent feelings. Ch'askancha was both thrilled and disappointed, thinking the much-needed discussion with his mother would be delayed and might not even happen that night.

"Ch'askawani, can you just help me remove the sacks on the alpacas so I can put the llamas in the corral with the alpacas?" *Asiri* immediately requested. Without hesitation, his grandson quickly stood and snagged his poncho hanging near the door. At the same time, Ru'qu shouted, "Tayta, when done, stay for a meal. We have plenty. Besides, you won't have to prepare anything for yourself."

Ru'qu knew her tayta would appreciate a meal already prepared, knowing he was exhausted from the long walk and probably would not prepare himself a meal before retiring for the evening. Moreover, his wife, *Kuychi*, her mama, died of a rare lung condition the previous winter season, a huge emotional blow to Arisi. She was the love of his life. Then there was the inconvenience of no one to cook for him regularly. Of course, she could, but her tayta didn't want that. In addition, Ru'qu recalled he had told her shortly after his wife's death, "I enjoy and prefer living alone."

9

Arisi responded to his daughter's invitation for a meal with a big smile, saying, "Thank you, love of my life. I'm tired, but a good warm meal before bed with good company is just what this old man needs to sleep well." As he finished his statement, he turned from the door opening and disappeared with Ch'askancha following him into the darkness that had descended on the village.

"Glad you are back, awki (grandfather)," the youngster said as he threw his arms around Arisi.

His grandfather giggled in reply and added, "Thank you, dear boy. You are wonderful. Others will know this in time, even you!"

Like pals, Arisi with his arm across his grandson's shoulder, Ch'askancha's arm around his awki's waist, the two walked to the corral.

Ch'askancha's eyes quickly adjusted to the darkness. He saw the two llamas, loaded with cargo. They were taller and weighed more than twice as much as the alpacas. Seeing the llamas reminded him of their usefulness as he had learned from awki Arisi. Besides being bred as pack animals, the llama's independent-mindedness made them excellent guard animals watching over other came-lids. As sure-footed as mountain goats, they were dependable in various terrains. Moreover, these camelids were old friends with Ch'askancha's ancestors, who domesticated the llama several millennia before the boy's time.

Once Arisi and his grandson had removed the sacks secured to the wooden frame packs, they unburdened the two llamas of the pack frames and released them into the corral to mingle with the alpacas. Asiri hoisted one sack over his shoulder and dragged another while Ch'askancha followed, pulling the remaining sack.

Once the sacks were secured in his grandfather's house, Arisi and Ch'askancha had finished their work. A wind had picked up, making the temperature more chilling. Grandpa and grandson walked briskly to the hot meal that awaited them.

Just before entering the partially open door, where smoke was still escaping along the top edge of the doorframe, Arisi grabbed his grandson by the forearm, stopping him, and said, "Thank you for helping. You are appreciated!"

Ch'askancha, having great respect for his awki, responded shyly but happily, smiling, and quickly turning his eyes away.

Inside, Ru'qu had prepared another place setting for her tayta. The family of three sat on the log, ate, laughed, and shared experiences of common interest that had consumed the last five days.

After the meal, all sipped chicha, a fermented beverage made from blue corn. Asiri had grabbed a gourd full and brought it from his house. All the villagers drank this "beer" to relax their bodies after a day's labor in the fields.

Ch'askancha sipped very little as he didn't like the taste.

His awki told him how it was made, which surprised the boy, "I make *chicha* by mashing blue corn and adding spit. The spit adds what is needed to ferment the mash and gives a slight buzz when I drink it."

"Spit, awki?" Ch'askancha questioned, expressing an intense distaste and aversion.

In good humor, Arisi laughed and let the conversation go.

After eating was finished, Ch'askancha stacked the bowls and pots to await cleaning and sterilization with hot water in the morning. Next, papa peelings scattered in front of where all three had sat would get cleaned up as an entertaining activity, common to the Quechuans. Ru'qu, looking toward the bed at the far end of the room, called out, "Eeeeeep. Eeeeeep."

A choir of Guinea pigs responded instantly, Eeeeeep. Eeeeeep. Squealing, they came running from beneath the bed. They swarmed over the papa peelings. The Guinea pigs did not stop eating until all the peelings vanished; then, they disappeared again under the bed.

More and more laughter erupted as Arisi repeated jokes he had heard while in Paucartambo, as the time that evening passed rapidly without notice. Finally, Arisi announced it was the day's end for him. The spirits of sleep were calling.

"Please, awki, one more joke," Ch'askancha begged.

"Alright," his awki conceded and began one last joke. "There was a young boy warmly snuggled in his bed covers. He dreamt of a young lad sitting in a grove of trees, noticing a figure moving in the distance. When he realized it was heading straight for him, he was unnerved. He continued to nervously stare and noticed the figure walking upright like any human. As it got closer, he saw whatever it was had hair all over its body, as it wore no clothes. The boy was becoming frightened. This "thing," whatever it was, was incredibly tall. Feeling his life in danger, he wanted to get up and run, but his body froze in place. He was terrified as the creature stood over. It was taller than the highest tree. The boy, beside himself with fear, asked the giant, 'What are you going to do to me?' The giant bent down, furrowed his eyebrows, and replied in a deep voice, 'I don't know; it's your dream!'

Ru'qu roared in laughter. So did Arisi. Ch'askancha, on the other hand, had an unexpected response of indifference. It reminded him too much of his dreams. Arisi noticed his grandson's cold reception to the joke but decided not to respond. It was getting late. Instead, he thanked his daughter and grandson. "What a great end to a long day. It was a delight spending this time together. I love you both," Arisi said, hugging both. Out the door he went, disappearing into the night, homeward bound.

The evening had reached a close. The flames from the hearth fire had all but disappeared, and heat currents gently rose. Ru'qu closed the door. The little smoke remaining seeped into the dense layers of hatched roofing, adding to the carbon layers already coating the rafters and ceiling. The house was in darkness except for the area immediately around the hearth where Ru'qu and Ch'askancha sat in silence in the dim light, resting and reliving different parts of the evening as memories. Each was in their thoughts without the need to speak.

Now..., Ch'askancha thought to himself, now maybe it is time for the story I've been waiting to hear that would answer so many of my questions. He glanced over at his mother, who was staring at the hot coals, her face flickering orange colors cast on her by the glowing coals.

"Mama, I want to know!" he blurted out, unable to contain the emotions building inside.

Surprised at her son's outburst, Ru'qu flinched. But she psychically knew the unspoken topic at hand. Moreover, she was expecting it, having focused on him during the day, feeling the emotional torment Ch'askancha was experiencing, and what had been through his dreams.

In her compassionate way, Ch'askancha's mother responded, "Son, I understand how you are feeling. I planted a seed of curiosity in you three years back, and it has grown to overshadow your emotions and thoughts. Forgive me for letting this fester like an open wound. It is probably all you can think about lately. You can be at ease to know I feel you are prepared to receive the full story. Your attention is strongly focused on the matter."

"You are right, mama," her son acknowledged, "So please tell me as much as you can. I do feel I can understand what you will say, and can accept it." His words reflected his exhaustion with the issue and his impatience too.

"Good," Ru'qu replied, "as that's my intention, and I will begin now."

Ch'askancha took a deep breath to exhale all the tension that had built up and was swirling in him. His mother took a deep breath to create a more relaxed atmosphere so she could tell him calmly, rather than excitedly rush past details that may be important. But, in the end, she knew her words would include only a summary of a tremendous life experience that was still unfolding. So, with a complete exhale, she began the long-awaited telling.

"What I am about to tell," Ru'qu said, "is full of surprises, some of which you already know.

Ch'askancha, thinking he knew nothing, begged, "What do I already know, mama?"

"You know of the landing of the Ch'usaq Pacha (celestial 'gods') from Ch'aska (the brightest star in the night sky, Sirius) at the sacred lake in the mountains."

"Yes, mama," the boy replied quickly, impatiently.

"You know the Ch'usaq Pachas left a baby boy with our people to be raised and, in doing so, entered him into the life cycle of Birth-Death-Birth in this world."

Ch'askancha said, "Yes," confirming the answer by nodding his head.

"You know that this baby was named Ch'askawani (Star Eyes) and grew up to be a great healer," Ru'qu continued.

"Yes, mama, but what does this folklore have to do with me not having a father?" Ch'askancha asked, puzzled about how it applied to his situation.

Ru'qu took a deep breath and spoke in an even tone, "My son, you did have a father. Your father was Ch'askawani!"

Unable to contain his emotions, the boy jumped up from his seat and yelled, "What, Mama? How can this be?" The words echoed in his mind.

The boy's eyes darted in all directions as if following the echoing thoughts. Ch'askancha was in a mild state of shock. Of all the possibilities he imagined over time of whom his mother would say was his father, the great Ch'askawani was not one of them.

Ch'askancha began to cry; he needed comfort. Who better than his loving mother? Finally, he fell to his knees before her and laid his head in her lap. Then, sympathizing, she quietly stroked Ch'askancha's thick, longish, black hair and patted him on the back while repeating, "It's alright. I understand. I love you dearly. It's alright..."

Her son's tears were tears of joy. But she also knew he was undergoing an energy shift, accepting this new information.

After many moments, Ch'askancha lifted himself and looked directly into his mother's shining blue eyes as tears continued to trickle down his cheeks, admitting, "Mama, I am so happy to be the son of such a great man. Thank you for telling me. I am so grateful for my life."

Ru'qu embraced him tightly and said, "I am so happy for you. To have a father who was a light being is an auspicious beginning for your life. To follow in his footsteps would be a life worth living. Ch'askawani showed us many things about life that have changed those who wanted to receive his messages; the essential news is to love yourself and everyone else.

Ch'askancha's thoughts were moving fast, probably too fast.

"Mama, where is Ch'askawani now? Is he dead, or has he gone someplace else? The folklore doesn't indicate. Why is that? Someone must know! Knowing he is my father carries me off into the heavens. A feeling I cannot explain, I didn't even ever imagine. But I am brought back down to Earth by those unanswered questions.

Ru'qu remained silent, only listening. Because the moment was causing her more emotional discomfort than anticipated, reliving memories of the horrifying night of Ch'askawani's murder, a fact Ch'askancha did not yet know.

Without a response, Ch'askancha continued. "It all seems a little strange; no one wants to talk about what happened to him. Villagers sing great praises to Ch'askawani, but when I ask what happened to him, they ask if I have talked to you about it. When I tell them you have refused to say anything until I am old enough to understand, they're not only reluctant, but they also flatly refuse to say anything. 'Talk to your mother' is the stock answer. So, Mama, what happened to Ch'askawani?"

The time for revelation had come. Ru'qu choked momentarily, tears filling her eyes.

"Mama, what is it?" Ch'askancha begged.

"I thought talking about Ch'askawani's death would get easier over time, but it hasn't...."

"So, he died," Ch'askancha concluded. Pleasure faded from his face, replaced with a look of misery.

"Son, he was murdered!" Ru'qu cried aloud. Then immediately put her face in her hands and sobbed helplessly, rocking back and forth.

"What?" Ch'askancha said, with tightened facial muscles. Then, he compassionately reached for his mother. He said nothing but only held her to comfort her, knowing the relief it had given him.

It took a while before Ru'qu settled down again. Then, regaining composure, she said, "I'm ok now," and started to explain, "Eleven years ago, two men savagely murdered Ch'askawani and Waywa one night at the beginning of the rainy season. From what we could figure, the men had come to the village from Qosqo to establish residency here. They came to the village, planning to include Sonqollaqta in the Inca Empire, which opposed the independent Ch'askawani's ideas and spiritual teachings. So, they decided to do away with him, and that, unexpected by them, did away with them. They fled that night in the driving rain and have never been seen or heard from again."

Ch'askancha asked, "Where did such a thing happen?"

"The murder occurred at the compound where Ch'askawani lived, which you know as the ruins outback," she indicated.

"I knew it," Ch'askancha shouted, "I had a feeling something horrible had happened there. What happened to the compound? The charred wood remains suggest someone burned it down."

More surprises were on the way for Ch'askancha.

Ru'qu's look of embarrassment led Ch'askancha to ask, "Mama, did you burn down the compound?" Then, again, he displayed his youthful eagerness of frank curiosity.

The question hung between them, lazily revolving. Finally, Ru'qu confessed, "I am about to tell you what I've never told anyone, not my father or mother, not even Chaskawani. I had no idea such a thing was possible."

Squinting, her son asked, "Mama, what are you talking about?"

"For me, the weeks following the funeral services for Ch'askawani and Waywa were filled with bouts of depression and fits of anger. One of those days when rage seemed in possession of me, I walked over to the compound. In doing so, memories of the dreadful night further enhanced the madness, as if I had done so deliberately.

"I was standing just inside the door when, suddenly, like a fish underwater, shooting up out of the water, a vengeful rage surfaced. My feelings got totally out of hand after having tried to suppress them for so long.

"I felt mean and wanted revenge. But I was masking my helplessness to change what had happened and move on. I was like a rat cornered by life's circumstances and had no other recourse than to attack. I remembered my eyebrows furrowed and face tightened.

"There alone, I started shouting at length in a wild, impassioned way—my body temperature rising rapidly at the same time. I got sweltering, like a temperature when sick, but much higher. I became delirious and thought I was hysterical at that moment and wondered if the rage was causing me to go insane. My body trembled as I felt waves of hot air radiating from my body. Then, unexpectedly, I sniffed that faint smell of smoke and heard a muffled *whrrr-rump* sound above me. As I looked up, the thatch of feathergrass had spontaneously burst into flames. I shrunk back, turned, and ran out to a safe distance. From there, I watched as the entire underside of the roof first issued smoke, and then the fire spread across the whole rooftop. Before long, the roof superstructure collapsed in a roaring blaze.

"I watched the entire compound as it burned and realized I was laughing a maniacal laugh simultaneously. *This laughter is crazy,* I thought, *who was I punishing? The building is on my family's property.* I felt like an idiot. What was I doing? Then I wondered, *Am I doing anything? I couldn't explain what had happened other than describing what I felt and what I saw.* Had I done anything? I couldn't say.

"Then the idea occurred that I had created a memorial that would be visible every day to every villager as a reminder of the great man who was taken from us needlessly.

"I knew there was only one way to determine if I had lit the compound on fire. So, I walked directly to the house Guari had built. I stood in front of the door, then decided to back up to a safe distance in case a similar eruption of smoke and flames occurred. Since Guari was most certainly the one who masterminded the killings, my hatred and anger toward him exploded in my mind. I felt like I was going crazy again, but there was also a feeling of power in it. The body heat ramped up quicker than before. This time, the fire started with the front door. I saw smoke coming from the boards on the door. Then that sound again, *whrrr-rump*. The door was instantly in flames, and the roof above it too.

"I stood fixed and watched the roof fall in with a sense of satisfaction that burned all the hatred out of my heart and mind. Seeing it to the end, I remained until there were only hot ashes. The house and its contents were several piles of rubble."

That day I regained my composure and sanity.

"So, the answer to your question is, yes. I lit the fire, but not how you think."

"Wow, Mama! You're a powerful being in your own right," Ch'askancha said proudly.

"But let us return to Ch'askawani. As you probably have wondered, Son, Ch'askawani knew the thoughts of those in his presence. He was aware trouble was brewing. He knew the villagers who were happy being just followers. They wanted to be him, to replace him. He knew the ugly face of jealousy and envy."

"If Ch'askawani knew this, why did he allow it to happen?" Ch'askancha asked.

"I asked him a similar question. I wondered why his psychic ability to foresee events couldn't help him avoid harm."

"This great man replied immediately, 'We live each life, in many ways, with events pre-planned in the spiritual realm. Events happen so we can learn from them; otherwise, what's the purpose. Life is only a joy ride for the ignorant, or so the ignorant think.

'If I am hurt, do not think the worst of those involved. Those who harm us can only do so by our agreement. All of those involved know about it and have agreed to it. There is something to be learned in every life situation. But, of course, when coming into the physical realm, we forget these agreements; yet they remain in place.

'To you and others, the lesson for will be known after the experience, if you contemplate the matter and ask the spirits for guidance. Life is full of happenings you can neither control, prevent nor make. So, understand how you respond to anything, all of life, and you will have a clue to your spiritual growth.'"

Ch'askancha could feel the emotion of his mother building and was not surprised to hear her cry out, "I can only imagine what it was like for Ch'askawani, psychically aware of his murder approaching. For me and poppy and mommy, it was terrifying to think the inevitable would happen."

The young boy was puzzled and said, "Mama, there must be something more to this story. Why would such an amazing man keep such a possibility like his own death to himself?"

"There is more to it yet to be told," was her response, adding, ``Here's the part that may seem odd to you. It explains you did have Ch'askawani as a father but goes beyond that to reveal who you are. I wasn't sure you'd be ready to hear what I am about to say, but the moment is here, and it's on the tip of my tongue."

The boy furrowed his eyebrows, wondering what this could be.

"Ch'askawani said he needed a means by which he, as spirit, after dropping his body, could reenter this physical world. He asked me if I would be that means! Trusting him as I did and knowing him to be flawless or faultless. That's how you happened."

Ch'askancha was speechless. The full impact of what his mother had just told him suddenly struck him like a lightning bolt of awareness.

Thinking about what his mother was about to say simultaneously, she said it.

"Long story short, you who are without a father are your father!"

TO BE CONTINUED

CPSIA information can be obtained
at www.ICGtesting.com
Printed in the USA
BVHW071503280822
645254BV00001B/38